I0831848

HIGH POINTS

HIGH POINTS

By

Aaron Coe

This Book Is
PUBLISHED BY LULU
(www.lulu.com)

First Edition: March 2020

ISBN 978-0-578-23195-2

Printed in the United States of America

ACKNOWLEDGMENTS

I'd like to acknowledge the many people whose names I've inserted and in some cases modified for some characters. These are friends or family members who helped with this novel or during my journalism career.–Adam Fyall, , a high-pointer and confirmed bachelor who lives life to the fullest to the envy of married guys, for his Facebook posts that inspired me to write this novel; My father, Michael Coe, for countless hours of proofreading. Deanna Riddle, Dayla Braunschweig and Sonja Wetzel for valuable feedback; Sam Cook, a retired Seattle Police Officer for insights; Larry Rosen for his guidance with self-publishing and document templates that saved me from drop-kicking my laptop; Former newspaper colleagues, including John "Mert" Marrs, Paul Archipley, Scott Johnson, John Sleeper and Chris Beatty for help and encouragement during my journalism days.

Dedication

To all those who volunteer their time to youth sports organizations, thank you for the hours you give. Your compensation comes in the form of seeing boys and girls grow into great men and women.

This book would not have been possible without the support of my mother, Deanna Riddle, and her husband, Bob Riddle, along with the tolerance and support of my wife Kathleen.

HIGH POINTS

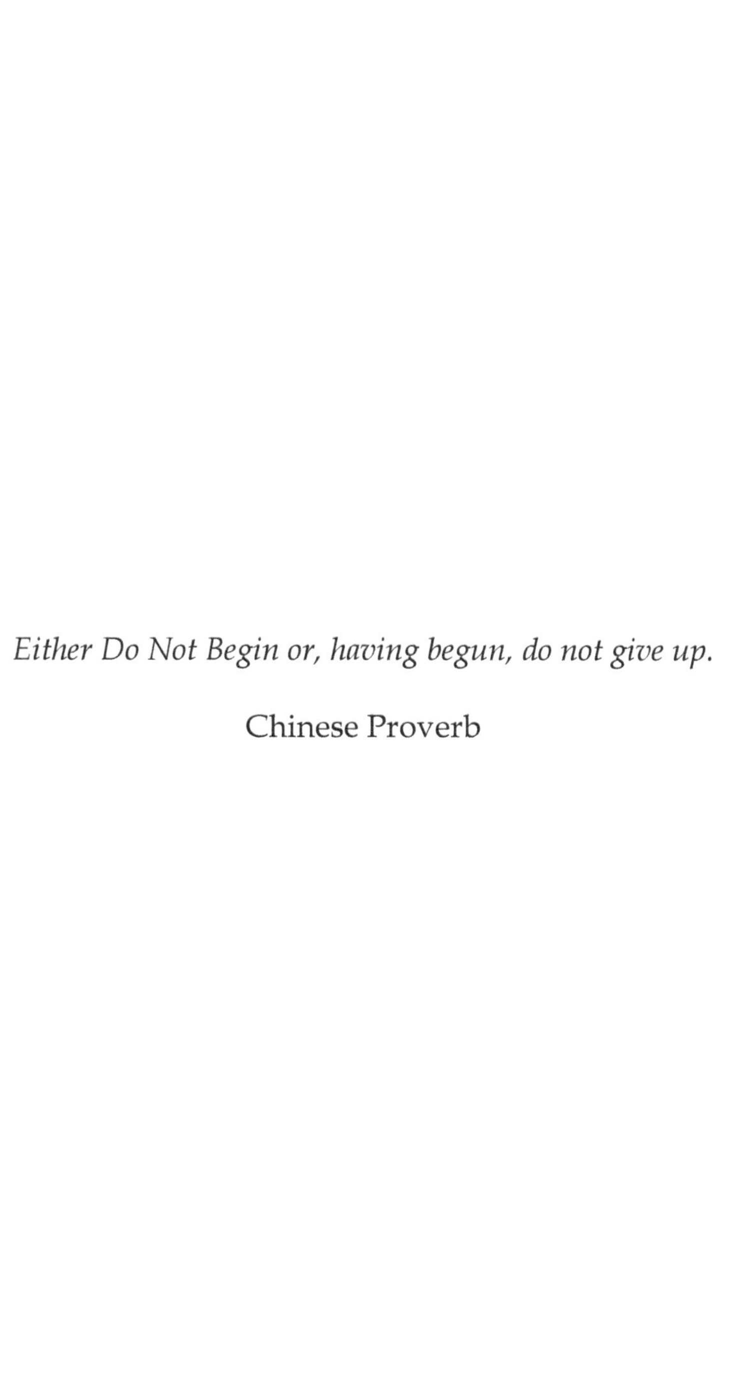

Either Do Not Begin or, having begun, do not give up.

Chinese Proverb

CONTENTS

CONTENTS
(Continued)

Part III: Bad Altitudes

Prologue

The Ozark Plateau, Arkansas

Women seem much heavier dead than alive.

With middle-aged knees aching, he lamented this revelation while lugging Tammy Weaver's lifeless body along the thickly-wooded trail. A blackjack oak shivered and moaned in the cool mountain breeze, causing him to freeze for a moment. He felt prepared for this hike, but the dead weight and the sounds emitted by the forest and its critters unnerved him.

Just past 2 a.m., alone and jittery, adrenaline prodded him along a trial run to see if this was going to be his thing.

Oh, and it was his thing. It was perfect in so many ways.

He reminisced the events of two hours ago, when her fake smile faded into lifelessness.

As her eyes showed the first hint of fear.

The moment when panic turned to acceptance.

When her eyes matched the emptiness of her soul.

Perfect.

But damn, 110 pounds felt heavy on this trail. Unprepared for the weight on his shoulders, he made a mental note to work his legs more at the gym. Every step burned a little deeper while offering the potential to be discovered, busted, jailed, bitch-slapped.

"No, focus, you idiot!" he whispered to himself as Tammy unwillingly nodded in agreement as her head bobbed with each of his steps. He reminded himself that he was ready for an unplanned encounter. He felt the pistol in his hiking jacket, though using it would lead to digging a hole for two.

He used anger to combat fatigue and fear. What was that sound?! A mountain lion? The police? Some crazed, toothless inbred mountain man? He took a deep breath and gathered himself as adrenaline seemed to ooze from his pores.

He remembered why he was here. She deserved this ending to her life of self-promotion. Braggadocious bitch. Another who used social media to pat herself on the back so hard she bruised.

That's where he found her. Who needs dark alleys and shadows? He'd stalked her online, hiding behind his computer monitor while she posted her every move on Facebook. He knew which days she volunteered at her kids' schools, when she met "the mom squad!" for coffee each week and what her ass looked like on a Maui beach.

Death promised to bring her what she'd wanted from life: Her face, everywhere. She was about to go viral. News stories about her disappearance would soon lead the evening news, he conceded. Scenes of the search party looking for her remains, distortions of her contributions to society, eulogies, nostalgic bullshit about what a great mom she was, great wife, blah, blah, blah.

He veered off the trail where it bent to the left–first time in Arkansas but he'd remembered the spot from Google Earth–and stumbled across decaying leaves that littered the forest floor. Another 500 feet should do it. He picked his way through the thickening brush. Branches, like annoying kid brothers, poked him repeatedly. Finally the small clearing appeared in front of him, a lone empty stool at a bar. In the middle of the forest's bald spot, he dropped her to the ground as his thigh muscles seemed to say, "It's about damned time."

As he shoveled dirt, he looked over his shoulder at her and said, "You're about to be famous, bitch."

Part I
A Vast Wasteland

1

HIGH AND OUTSIDE

Freedom Field
Mill Creek, Washington

"Throw strikes!" she yelled at her 11-year-old for the third time. Great advice, I thought, as I sat on the ball bucket in the dugout with the brim of my hat touching the chain-link fence. The boy, who hadn't thrown many strikes that night, threw watery-eyed a glance at her that said, "No shit, mom."

We were down 11-0 in the second inning. Two more innings–an eternity when you're getting clobbered–until the mercy rule ended this episode of Field of Nightmares.

The truth is I cared about the kids on that team like they were my own. I'd stuffed them in the minivan and taken them to Mariners games and out for post-game treats at the place where you put a small layer of frozen yogurt in a cup and then bury it with 17 kinds of candy bars and cookies. I'd set up a Facebook account mostly so I could post silly selfies with them while also getting a glimpse of their lives outside the lines.

But, we all have days when we just aren't feeling it, and apparently this was mine. My thoughts drifted, only occasionally toward the game I was coaching.

I crossed my arms and hoped the kid's next pitch would be a strike. And, it was! Unfortunately, the strike was hit to our thick third baseman, whose throw sailed 10 feet over the first baseman's head and shook the fence bordering right field. Two errors later, the Red Sox had what we call a "mommy home run."

I was sure I'd see this on Facebook later: "Timmy hit a home run!" No, you annoying witch. Three errors does not equal a home run.

I looked up as the numbers on the electronic scoreboard changed. The ballpark lights began to glow as the sun lowered itself behind the Douglas fir trees beyond left field.

The pitcher's chest began heaving. Lovely. He was sobbing, and a single tear drifted down a freckled cheek. As I imagined Tom Hanks yelling, "There's no crying in baseball!" my assistant coach tapped me on the shoulder and said more than asked, "You want me to make a change, Bob?"

I nodded.

"Who do you want?" Dick asked.

"Anybody who can throw a damned strike."

He raised his eyebrows and turned toward the field.

As Dick consoled our pitcher with one arm and signaled in our center fielder to succeed him with the other, my mind drifted again. I thought about some of the people having more fun than me at this moment, sipping umbrella drinks on an island, attending a real baseball game or even just catching happy hour at the bar down the street. Or something crazy, like a nice dinner with a loved one? I couldn't remember the last time I'd given my wife a reason to wear her black dress.

I especially envied guys like my fellow high school alumnus, Jake Mallory. Why had Jake drifted into my mind at this exact moment? I tried to push him out of there, but just before pregame warmups I'd glanced at

Facebook. He was there, as usual, this time with a blonde twin on each arm. I couldn't shake the image.

Asshole.

I thought about my wife in the black dress again, and this time imagined she had a twin.

"Too much work," I said out loud, drawing a confused look from a kid on the bench as our new pitcher one-hopped a throw to the catcher.

There were moments when I wanted to be like Jake, but then I'd realize that I was just too damned tired.

The married 40-somethings I know, deep down, envy guys like this. Jake runs a marathon. We walk the dog and scoop its shit. Jake tracks down the boyhood home of blues legend Robert Johnson. We wince at a middle-school band concert. Jake climbs a mountain and "can't wait for the next challenge!" I feel dejected if an escalator breaks down.

I can't wait for one less challenge. I need a nap.

"Hey, let's keep it moving!" the other team's manager yelled at the umpire as Dick attempted to inspire both the pitcher and his replacement.

"Give it a rest, Smitty," one of the parents from my team shot back.

"Hey, I'm not getting' any younger over here," said Smith, loudly laughing alone.

Smith's kid was due up next, and I considered the ramifications of beaning a little kid. Probably less jail time than if I threw something at Smith's head.

The ump interrupted my thoughts by shouting, "Play ball!"

Our new pitcher, Kyle threw a pitch that looked good from the dugout, but the ump called it a ball.

"Hey, Blue, where was that one?" I shouted.

"I'll tell you where it wasn't, Bob: The strike zone."

"Everyone's a comedian today," I muttered.

Ball two. I scolded myself for thinking, "Throw strikes!"

Ball three. High and outside. I looked to the sky hoping for a downpour.

Ball four. Bounced and hit my catcher in his special place. Why is there a rule about no beer in the dugout?

With his kid now at first base, Smith went through his signs. In the midst of grabbing everything but his left testicle, I saw something that made my fists form into white-knuckled balls. No, he wouldn't call that, now, would he?

No, he must have changed his signs, which I'd stolen last game. Not even Smith was that big of a horse's ass.

Kyle delivered a rare strike. Smith's kid paused and then took off for second base as our catcher casually tossed the ball back to the pitcher. Delay steal with an 11-run lead. He *was* that big of an ass.

I glared at Smith, and he smiled back, arrogantly.

"Hey, you guys gotta watch for that!" a parent yelled from the stands.

"Come on, boys!" hollered another mom.

"That's just poor coaching," a dad grumbled.

Orphans, I thought. Maybe even fantasized. Wouldn't it be great to coach orphans? No murmurs from the stands. No whining about playing time. No social media stupidity.

Orphans. That's what I need. A team of orphans.

I rested my elbows on the crossbar of the dugout fence and watched Kyle throw four straight balls.

Black dress. I needed to give Kathleen a reason to wear that dress.

Dick interrupted that thought, stepping halfway out of the dugout and looking at me, his nonverbal way of asking if he could talk to the pitcher. I nodded, and he asked the ump for time as a light rain began to fall. The shivering parents in the stands groaned in disapproval.

Of course if my kids were orphans, I wouldn't be here. I'd be–well, maybe I'd be like Jake Mallory, dousing others' Facebook feeds with my exploits.

If not for the Internet–and more specifically, Facebook–I wouldn't know a post-high-school thing about Jake Mallory. I might have pictured him with a few gray hairs sprouting in the mini-mullet grown 25 years ago. A person's hairstyle remains forever frozen in time if you never see them again. Just think Chachi from Happy Days. Or Farrah Fawcett.

Thanks to Facebook, I learned everything about Jake. No wife to slow him. No kids, no bills and seemingly fewer concerns than my Labrador Retriever. Another thing they had in common, I suspected, was that they both humped everything in sight.

Anyone in the world with Internet access can find all kinds of interesting facts about Jake. Or me for that matter, if anything about me interested anyone. The way things turned out, that's one big strike against the Internet in my mind.

"Stri-eeeke," the ump hollered as Kyle painted the corner shortly after Dick's return to the dugout.

"Where was that one?" Smith asked.

"That one was in the strike zone, Smitty," the ump said.

Strike two, followed by a slow roller to the first baseman, the safest play in baseball. As Bill Buckner learned in the 1986 World Series, however it's never a sure thing. Our first baseman performed his best Buckner, and the ball rolled between his feet and into the outfield. Smith's kid raced home for his team's 12th run with parents rolling their eyes in perfect unison. I stood silently.

After we eventually got out of the inning, I gave a half-assed pep talk that included some B.S. about "no mountain being too big to climb."

If I only had the balls to climb a real mountain. As I stood at third base giving signs that meant nothing, I pictured myself climbing with Jake. His chiseled body side-by-side with my pudgy one.

Were we so different? I could climb mountains, party with strippers and shoot par on a golf course, right? We could tag each other in our Facebook posts. Wouldn't that be cute?

As it turned out, we did end up spending some time together. If I could go back in time and unfriend that guy… .

2

Frenemies

Home, Semi-Sweet Home

Rhonda Corwin, annoying baseball mom, Facebook post: Great pitching by Timmy today! We almost made it to the championship game! The boy's played hard! Just one to many mistake's today!

A few days after coaching the Bad-News-Bears-style fiasco, a select baseball team I coach played in a tournament. It all went well, other than one play by my kid at the end.

Home after the tough loss, I sat down with a cold beer and scrolled Facebook, finding Rhonda Corwin's unpleasant reminder as rain began to pelt my over-the-hill roof. Rhonda, my Facebook frenemy, serial apostrophe rapist and wearer of the slightly too tight T-shirt that says "Some people never meet a baseball star. I raised mine!" Dumb as she was, she was a genius when it came to not-so-hidden messages.

Why don't you just say it, Rhonda? "If Bob Peddin's kid hadn't pissed away the game by bobbling that ball, my future middle-management suck-up would be in the championship game!"

If I'm good at anything, it's translating Facebook posts. I can read between the phony half-sentences and tell you what every 40-something is really saying. Secret meanings hid behind every one of Rhonda's posts like snipers taking shots at little kids and their parents. She masterfully wrote posts that technically contained nothing negative but forced readers to finish her sentence with some sort of insult of themselves. She implied the "but" that erased any good will that came from the part you could actually read. Kind of like when people start a sentence with, "No offense, but… ." Maybe that's what angered me the most. She used our own ugly thoughts against us.

She had a pretty face and long blonde hair that drew the attention of men and women. I guessed it took a pit crew to get her hair and makeup ready for the day. She also had a big, fat ass. Not J-Lo big. That's good big. More like Grimace from McDonald's big. When she wore purple, I expected the Hamburglar to join her at any moment.

One of the best decisions I ever made was when I recently decided I'm done with people like her. We all get a limited number of days on this earth. After all that's happened, I prefer to live a Rhonda-free lifestyle.

My wife, Kathleen, clanged pans together in the kitchen, a reminder that my place was in the kitchen just as much as hers. I shifted my weight to get up, but didn't quite gather the momentum–mentally more than physically–to complete the move.

I looked at Rhonda's post again. I reread the post, and the mouse hung over the "like" button for an eternity…

Decisions like this are excruciating. To like this Facebook post would be tacit approval of her backdoor jab at my son. To pass up a like, though, could be seen as a metaphorical, passive-aggressive stabbing in the neck of little Timmy. Revenge for mentioning my son's costly error, but unforgiveable by every mom who counts "likes."

I considered this important decision as auto body shop-like noises emanated from the kitchen.

"Need any help?" I asked, bracing myself.

"Yeah, if you're not too busy," Kathleen sighed.

I explained my dilemma to Kathleen, but she seemed to think she had more important things to deal with at that moment.

I swear, an unwritten rulebook exists for Facebook "likes." If I never, ever liked anything, I'd be in the clear. "He just doesn't like anything. He probably doesn't even know you can do that." If you like everything, then you are a like-slut, indiscriminately liking everything without realizing how cheap and meaningless each one of your likes has become.

For this reason, each Facebook user must thoughtfully determine the correct threshold a post must reach to earn one's "like." What is just funny, heartfelt or interesting enough? Will your decision not to exercise your "like" lead to wives fighting?

"Ahhhh, dammit," I sighed.

Like.

I threw my weight forward, scolded by my knee for its lack of cartilage, and limped to the kitchen.

"Bob, you had to like it," said Kathleen, my wife, shortly after being subjected to a verbal pro-con list of liking versus not liking my son's teammate's mom's Facebook status.

She handed me a plate with a sandwich and potato salad that appeared to have lived one day too long. I considered asking why there had been so much noise for a sandwich, but decided it would be better to outlive the potato salad.

"You have no idea how painful it was to like that."

"You had to. You're the coach of the team. Next time just like it right away and save us both from ten minutes of our lives we'll never get back."

"Why did I have to like it, again?" I said, lowering myself back into the chair before taking a long pull on my beer.

"Because then there would be another post about how SOME people REFUSE to like things just because they're jealous," she said, offering an inquisitive glance to the potato salad on her plate. "And then every one of her friends will like that."

"Would you like that?" I asked, earning only a sideways glance.

I typed, "One of these day's Timmys going to get bludgeoned by his own baseball bat." in the comment line.

"What. Are. You. Typing?" Kathleen asked, half growl-half groan.

Sigh. I held down the backspace button.

3

ALONE TIME

Schenectady, New York

She was an active social media user, and for this he felt gratitude. He'd read about her in a local newspaper–she was making poor kids read and eat their vegetables. She'd held up well after having a couple of little shits. Face still relatively wrinkle-free and an ample chest that was alive and well, though it had moved a couple of degrees south.

Between her posts and her husband's tweets over the period of a few weeks, he calculated that Thursday at 7:45 was the time. Her husband played basketball with his work buddies. Her daughter, Isobel, danced the night away at SuperStar Dance Academy and her son Charlie laid basketball bricks in a gym 3 miles away from dad. He was doing them all a favor tonight.

If he'd calculated correctly based upon her last few weeks of Facebook posts, she planned to come home, pour herself a glass of red wine and watch her favorite reality TV show with no distractions. Soon those distractions would come home, motherless.

He parked on the street in front of a greenbelt bordered by a black fence, aware of the other houses full of potential witnesses. He preferred an isolated target, but this would have to do. The houses were a couple of decades old but well-kept. This wasn't one of the newer neighborhoods where a person had to use a treadmill regularly if he planned to fit between his house and his neighbor's. With neutral colors and stone trim, sprinkled amidst mature trees, they sat on 20,000-square-foot lots. Still the risk of being spotted existed.

He exited the rental car wearing black sweatpants, a dark green sweatshirt and a baseball cap. Nothing noticeable, but no so unnoticeable that it actually became noticeable again.

Approaching the house, he discreetly looked around for pedestrians and listened for cars. Nothing at the moment, so he picked up his pace and made a break for a large rhododendron adjacent to the garage.

His pulse quickened a bit. 7:43. Any minute now. 7:47. Cars passed, none of them hers. Where the hell was she?

Finally, at 7:49, he heard the garage opener grumble as it pulled the door up. He waited, looking around one more time for witnesses who would force him to go to his alternative, much messier plan. The timing for this would be crucial. The door started down and he forced himself to wait three seconds before rounding the corner and hurling himself through the shrinking opening.

She'd stepped out of the car and was glancing at her phone before entering the main section of the house. With his entry camouflaged by the noise of the garage door, he calmly walked behind her and jabbed the needle into her neck. She turned her head toward him as her wide eyes turned to nothingness.

Fucking clockwork. The best one yet. Now he just had to get her to her new home.

He laid her between the front of her SUV and garage shelving that appeared much too organized. He pushed the garage door opener and watched it rise along with his heart rate. A car passed as he slinked behind some shelving. Now clear, he feigned calmness as he returned to his rental. He pulled into the other side of the garage, lowered the door and moved her to the plastic-covered backseat.

He looked through the miniature, diamond-shaped garage-door windows and waited for a jogger to pass. He hit the garage door remote with his gloved hand, backed out and walked back into the garage. Looking out one last time, he pushed the garage door remote and sprinted a few steps before ducking under the closing door. Thankfully, it was an older unit that came without the annoying safety sensors that send doors back up in case you've accidentally set your infant under the door.

Back in the car, he saw headlights in the distance. Best to wait it out. As the SUV approached, he considered what police would investigate. Likely it would be a nondescript man walking down the street and a nondescript car (with stolen plates) in the driveway. Worst-case, someone saw the nondescript man entering or exiting the garage. Best case, no one saw a damned thing. The way people kept their noses in their phones these days, he'd bet on the latter.

With the street clear again, he began the hour-long drive to the trail.

4

NEW YORK STATE OF MIND

Keene Valley, New York

Jake Mallory Facebook post: Start Spreading the News, I just reached the summit of Mt. Marcy (highest natural point of elevation in New York state.)

Jake was climbing more mountains. A few years back he apparently decided he wanted to be a high pointer, a person who reaches the highest natural point of elevation in each of the 50 states. If you had nothing better to do, you could simply drive up to some of those high points, step out of your car and take your Facebook selfie. Others require gear, money and someone like Jake to make it to the top.

Me? No chance. I'm thinking of scaling the fence to get out of this summer school teaching job. I hate him.

Like.

Next post…

5

NEW YORK, NEW YORK?

Rhonda Corwin Facebook post: My heart goes out to the family of that Mom over in Skenecteddy New York. I hope they find her soon! I remember how freaked out my husband was when he couldnt find me for a couple of hour's!

She was doing it again, another failure of the education system. No one ever took her by the hand and showed her how apostrophes work. I typed, "Maybe next time he'll need a shovel to find you" into the comment line. Then, I slowly–and with a bit more force than necessary–hit the backspace button to erase each letter. I "liked" her post but didn't comment. I'm not even aggressive enough to be passive aggressive.

I looked at my Facebook feed again. Why, I don't know. It wasn't a habit as much as it was a reflex to fill any two seconds of down time. Funny that Rhonda and Jake both mentioned New York. Jake, would you consider dropping Rhonda off your next high point?

"Uhhh, what?" Kathleen asked.

"Oh, was that out loud?" I asked as she offered a loving smirk-smile. "Sorry, I'll do anything to get out of planning tomorrow's classes."

Kathleen is busy, too. We have a strong marriage, I think, though she probably mostly tolerates me. I'm kind of a pain in the ass. My brain won't shut off, which leads to bouts of insomnia and curmudgeonliness. Is that a word? Ah, who cares? These days we can all do whatever we want with words without fucking consequence.

My stubbornness occasionally got me in trouble with Kathleen and others. When I believed I was right, I would not let something go, even if it led to my own suffering. I often thought about how right I was while sleeping on the couch. Most people at some point realize that being right isn't worth the burden, though that is a lesson I've failed to learn despite countless opportunities. It's impossible to explain how I landed someone so beautiful, tolerant and forgiving.

Hmmmm, Jake in New York. Dead woman in New York.

Despite a ton of work to do, I was really stalling now by amusing myself with this mock conspiracy theory. Jake Mallory, mommy killer. I didn't have the time or energy to kill the mouse living in my garage, but I would certainly make the time to research this angle. Always curious about things that really should not impact my life in any way, that is the type of thing I did with a rare few moments to spare. Besides, the last time I'd tried to catch that mouse I'd chased it with a baseball bat while yelling, "Die, bitch, die!" Kathleen was amused by this, but also mildly annoyed that the neighbors likely heard.

My mind wandered back to the woman in New York, and drifted further as I thought for a moment about how horrible it would be for the kids and me to lose Kathleen. My defense mechanism when I started feeling emotion like that was to pull myself out of it with something slightly sick. I bet a guy with a sad face, dead wife and insurance check enjoys significantly increased odds of providing the meat in a sympathetic chick threesome sandwich, I thought.

Curiosity wasting my time again, I searched for an article about the missing woman in New York. It wasn't hard to find. Of course people die and go missing every day, but this woman was white, upper-middle class and attractive. A media darling trending on Twitter.

According to the newspaper report, she looked like a candidate for mother-of-the-year. Involved in her kids' school and the community. Active in her church, where she'd started some program where the rich kids make themselves feel good by bringing healthy snacks and books to kids on the wrong side of town.

I looked at a few of her photos. One of those women who probably was a six on the hot scale in high school but an eight these days, factoring in age. She'd held up well, and the chest she'd probably buried in oversized sweaters in the 1980s now had a chance to peek out, just enough to still be tasteful. I figured she was dead. A moment of silence, I thought, for another bust taken from us far too soon. Thoughts like that made me pretty sure I was a bad person.

6

DAWGIE STYLE

Seattle, Washington

My Facebook post: Pigging out Dawgie Style! –with Rich Gibson, Ashley Muehler and Jake Mallory.

Even I thought that post was gross. I'm not what you'd call a "selfie" kind of guy, but what the hell? I hadn't seen these folks in years. And, with an evening kickoff for the University of Washington Huskies football game, we'd had a beer or two (or seven) as we prepared to cheer on our beloved Dawgs against the Arkansas Razorbacks.

Much later than most of the party-goers, I parked far away and walked across the paved lot to Jake's prime location. Graying adults bounced around like college sophomores. The September Seattle sun shined above, showing itself one last time before its annual 9-month hibernation. The rays glinted off steel and aluminum at Husky Stadium, picturesque with Mount Rainier in the distance. A seaplane flew overhead, likely preparing to land on Lake Washington and moor in Husky Harbor. I wondered what makes a person want to land an airplane on water, climb into a tiny boat, then climb out and go to a football game. No thanks.

Jake hadn't flown in, but his pregame was an event months in the making. He would not be satisfied with grilling hot dogs. Because the home team was playing the Arkansas Razorbacks, he'd flown in an actual razorback pig, rented roasting equipment somewhere and had started preparing and roasting it the night before. All while dressed as Jed Clampett. Despite my deep fear of catching swine fever from the southern cuisine of this amateur, would-be hillbilly, I played along and ate this pig of questionable background.

Jake bounced from fan to fan. (I'm not sure if he viewed them as football fans or Jake fans.) Lots of back-slapping and belly laughs at jokes that would set off an all-points bulletin if the political correctness police ever heard them.

He stopped in front of me, just long enough to ask, "Hey, how do you circumcise an Arkansas football fan?"

He glanced at my deadpan face and decided not to wait for me to guess.

"Kick his sister in the jaw."

He laughed too hard at this, and moved along to his next victim.

A mingling minimalist, I had a beer in one hand and my iPhone in the other for those semi-fun but slow-moving hours. I hadn't seen–or really had any interest at all in seeing–many of these people since high school. For some reason Jake took an interest in some of my Facebook comments about the University of Washington football team and insisted I join Jake's Tailgating Experience.

These were high school/Facebook "friends." Not actual friends. The air quotes are crucial in these situations.

There was Rich Gibson, a decent high school athlete, and the most pompous ass I'd known in my youth. That's saying a lot, considering the stiff competition offered by Jake.

Rich stood 6-foot-2 to my 5-7. I did have a weight advantage, though. Rich, a runner these days, hadn't gained a pound since high school. He wore a purple golf shirt and khakis, looking like a member of the Huskies coaching staff from 20 years ago.

It wasn't really Rich's fault, though. His parents decided to call him Rich despite the many options available to a person named Richard. Sure, he could change it now, but the damage was done. He was a prick and there was no turning back.

When a parent chooses the name Richard there are many directions that kid can go. I'm convinced it has everything to with which derivation of Richard sticks. Here's how it works:

- Richard: This name doesn't stick often unless the surname is followed by "the third." Richard never goes by Rich, but he is rich. Old money. A quiet confidence. Never flamboyant. Works hard but never gets his hands dirty. Richard decides you're fired but isn't the one to tell you. He also makes donations to charitable organizations without inviting news cameras. It's for the tax write-off, not the publicity. Rich doesn't need the publicity, he's got it all.
- Rick: A likeable guy who's always up to something with blurred legality. Rick always has a deal for you. He won't totally screw you over, but you can bet he's working an angle that benefits him. He saves you five bucks, but he's making a hundred. But, you still like him even though you know this. At least once a day,

someone thinks about Rick and utters, "Ahhhhh, Rick."

- Ricky: Watch out for any Ricky over the age of five. He will steal your stuff and sell it to your mother. Your mom loves Ricky–he's always smiling–and has no clue that he's a total shitbag. He would definitely fuck your mother and sell it to a porn site if given the chance.
- Dick: Usually 85 years old. Dick is not a dick. He's a trustworthy, humble guy who will help you with a brake job and then make you a bologna sandwich. This is a dying breed of man. Everyone needs a Dick.
- Rich: This is actually the dick of the bunch. Rich believes he's better than everyone, despite usually being just above average. He's sure he is always right, and no one will ever accumulate enough evidence to change his mind even if he's dead wrong. Never, ever, get into a political discussion with Rich. He always wears polo shirts. Add the khaki shorts for summer. Add a sport jacket for formal, but never remove the polo. Don't play golf with Rich. He will break out the rulebook on you and add shots to your scorecard. If Richard decides to fire you, Rich is the one he sends to do the deed.

My conversation with Rich Gibson lasted just long enough for us to come to an understanding that he had a better job, more athletic kids and a wife with bigger tits (helped by a plastic surgeon, I suspected). He threw in the play-by-play of his most recent round of golf. He'd birdied the last hole to beat his buddy out of 50 bucks. I told him about the time I got a hole-in-one but it wasn't the right hole. I'd hit hard, but so poorly that it crossed over one fairway and rolled into the cup while someone attempted a putt. Probably the coolest thing I'd ever seen on a golf course. Without as much as a fake smile, he moved on to the story about how he would have had an ace if the groundskeeper had done a better job with the greens that day.

What a dick.

I escaped to piss on a tree, only to be blindsided by Ashley Muehler as I zipped up and turned around.

I was trapped for 47 excruciating minutes. Ashley's a high-functioning nut job. I had to "hide" her on Facebook almost immediately due to political rants and excessive whining. I got the full run-down on all of her illnesses. The word around the roasted pig was that most were likely feigned. Next she explained how the school was fucking over her children. Those damned teachers! She told me about her ex-husband. He was apparently an asshole, but somehow I walked away just feeling sorry for him. I would certainly be an asshole if I spent one more minute with her.

In between games of beer pong and corn hole, I found myself again standing next to Jake. I broke a semi-awkward silence with something that led to full-blast awkwardness.

"Hey, how's your mom? She still living in that house?"

Jake paused long enough to plant, water and grow a big smile, and said, "She doesn't live anywhere. She died four years ago."

Fuck. Now what, Bob? This is exactly why I don't talk to people.

"Uh, she was, uh, a nice woman," I said, scolding myself even more after allowing a brief memory of Jake's mom's 1985 cleavage to sneak into my consciousness.

"Yeah, thanks."

"Uh, how did she, uh, uh," I said with Jake waiting for my word choice. "How did she pass?"

"Accident," was all he said.

That was enough for me. I begged anyone who could hear my thoughts to somehow distract Jake so he would walk away, but we stood there in silence for 30 seconds that felt like 30 minutes.

A few feet away, a drunken female fellow grad caught a football, then was mock-tackled–more like pawed–by a guy who was not her husband. They collapsed to the ground, giggling. He pretended to try to steal the football, but his hands seemed to find other round objects. I figured their marriages might soon take a turn. He helped her up and they swerved away. That's the thing about night games. Lots of time to drink and no real reason to think.

Back to Jake, who for some reason hadn't found someone more interesting.

"I see you've been scaling some mountains," I said, reaching for the only subject that came to mind.

"Yeah, a boy's gotta have a hobby," he said grabbing two bottles of beer from a cooler that sat behind a mid-70s Cadillac convertible. I remembered the car, his mother's baby. She allowed him to borrow that barge-sized behemoth for prom. It was amazing how many assholes you could fit in that thing. For today's game, he'd added a magnetized purple W to each side of the car along with flags and some other purple stuff to go with the car's gold paint. It was the perfect car to drive to a U-dub football game. Of course it was.

Jake looked me at me with his brown eyes. So dark they appeared all pupil. Ah, those eyes. I don't know what it was, but it always felt like those eyes could see through my skin and into the inner-workings of my soul. Like he knew what I was thinking, but that what was on my mind just wasn't all that interesting. Like a surfer who began to paddle before realizing the wave was no more than ankle slop.

Jake told me about some of his adventures. I listened off and on–just enough to ask follow-up questions while sipping free beer. It wouldn't be the last free beer from Jake, though the circumstances today were far different.

Jake, of course, had brewed the beer himself, using hops he'd planted on a friend's property in eastern Washington. He'd designed and printed his own label, which featured a woman who could have been the St. Pauli girl's hardened, brunette sister. He named his masterpiece "Dawgie-style" Ale.

Jake had already asked the obligatory "how are the wife and kids?" questions even though he probably saw them as weights that pulled down my shot at his hot-air balloon life. He made a solid effort to talk about me, but it's hard to keep a conversation going when the topic is that boring.

"So, how was Mt. Marcy?" I asked, when I couldn't think of anything else.

"You know, it was a little bit more challenging than I thought it would be. Nothing like some of the stuff west of the Rockies, but it wasn't easy."

"It was funny. I saw your stuff on Facebook, and then there was all that stuff about that woman from Schenectady." I stifled a Dawgie-style ale burp and wondered why I'd said such an uninteresting thing. There was some part of me that still wanted to impress this guy, something I'd failed to do in high school. It surprised me how type-cast we all were to each other all these years later.

Jake, watching a stream of sorority girls stumble toward the stadium, paused. Just a little pause, like a dog freezing for a moment to see if he'd actually heard a noise worth checking out. He turned slowly toward me, those dark eyes looking directly into mine.

"Yeah I remember that was all over the news–must've been a slow news day," he said, waiting a moment for me to hold up my end of the conversation.

Sensing I had nothing, he finished with, "They'll probably never find her."

I don't know why, but those eyes seemed even darker. I felt a chill from the Seattle September evening breeze. At least I thought it was the breeze.

He held my gaze for just long enough for it to be weird, then answered a call for a turn at the beer pong table.

PART II
HIGH ABOVE SUSPICION

7

Paper Boys

Mallory Facebook post: I'm feelin' a little loopy after cresting Guadalupe (Texas)!. 41 High Points down, 9 to go!!

That's what greeted me as I sat down in my La-Z-Boy with a beer in one hand and my phone in the other. It was baseball season, and the end-of-the-school year teacher push was in full swing. I felt like used coffee grounds. I resembled something useful, but I was spent.

I hadn't seen Jake since that UW game last fall. He'd been to Cabo, Vegas and a few other places since then, but this was his first high point since last fall.

That spring afternoon, I'd stumbled through the front yard just long enough to hold off the neighborhood association for a while. That lawnmower and I battled hard, jaggedly cutting through a few weeks of April growth. Until we meet again next month.

I decided to leave the hedge trimmer untouched and catch some baseball on TV. "Sorry, old man Hanks," I mumbled to myself, thinking about my obsessive-compulsive landscaping neighbor, whose hatred toward me began with the condition of my front yard. Today, the stars had aligned, and I planned to enjoy a precious free two hours. Kathleen and the kids were gone. I couldn't remember where, and knew I'd need to figure it out later so I could pretend like it was interesting. Play dates?

Curing cancer? Whatever. Silence. For two hours. My desert island.

I flipped on the TV, needing to kill a few minutes before the Mariners game. I'd better watch them now. Might never have another chance. And, it was April, and there was still hope that they might not suck this year.

I wasn't going to get up for any reason. I juggled a beer, my phone and the remote, landing on the national news, Facebook and a damned good IPA.

Facebook had again adjusted the way the feed presents itself, and at the top of the feed was a photo of Jake's Guadalupe Peak summit even though he'd posted it a week earlier. "Bite me, Jake," I muttered to myself.

I quickly scrolled through Facebook posts, my phone serving as a treadmill for my thumbs, pausing when necessary.

Rhonda Facebook check-in a T-Mobile Park: "Go Ms!"

Like. Comment only for the purpose of fixing her missing apostrophe. "Have fun at the M's game!" I knew my back-door teaching method would fail and Kathleen would likely scold me later for trying.

Stanley, a recovering addict well on his way to unrecovering: "After all I've done, this is how I'm treated."

No like. Can't chance it, even if there's only a one percent possibility that he might open up to me.

Piano recital video everyone would "like" without ever watching it.

Like.

I thumbed through the Facebook feed, pausing only for the occasional "like."

The TV grabbed my attention.

"An El Paso community remains stunned today, nearly a week after the disappearance of beloved PTA president and mother of three, Jill Collins. Collins left her Glenview neighborhood home for a PTA meeting on Tuesday, never arriving."

"That's not at all like her to miss a meeting," said a frumpy face belonging to Christy Campbell, Glenview Elementary PTA treasurer.

I thought about Jake's trip to Texas at the same time the woman disappeared.

Not this again. Stop it. You don't know a guy who kills moms. A serial killer. I chuckled at the silly connection made by my overactive and often under-stimulated brain.

El Paso, TX.

Guadalupe Peak.

According to Google Maps, about 111 miles apart.

"Her car was found…" squawked a news reporter, who didn't seem smart enough or hot enough to have a TV media job. You have to be one or the other, though hotness usually wins.

"Police are looking for…"

Then, another voice, one in my head said, "They'll probably never find her."

To dark eyes that weren't there, I said, "You're probably right."

"You're just being an idiot," I said to myself for even thinking about Jake, the beginning of an argument I would have with myself for months.

"I don't believe in coincidences."

I remembered that line came from LAPD Detective Harry Bosch, a recurring character in Michael Connelly novels I loved to read. Bosch, like any real or imaginary detective, felt compelled to follow each coincidence to its beginnings, usually determining that it wasn't a coincidence after all.

"You're no Harry Bosch."

"So, housewives just magically disappear every time Jake goes up a hill?" I questioned myself.

"Jake and Jill go up the..."

"Dude, really?"

"What are the odds that you know a serial killer?"

"Probably not good, but doesn't *someone* have to know each serial killer?"

"Yeah–again, what are the odds?"

"Not good, but…"

But, do those odds increase when you consider Jake's shitty childhood?

My mind drifted back to junior high, when I learned some things about Jake that, at least back then, very few people knew.

Jake and I both happened to move to the same neighborhood in the middle of seventh grade. The junior high world had already been sorted into Preps, Rockers, Wavers and Nerds. There was an unorganized miscellaneous group that included Jake and me. People who moved in during the middle of the school year found themselves in this social-group waiting area. I bought an alligator shirt and slowly crept toward the lower rungs of the Preps.

Jake bounced around for a while, trying different wardrobes and personalities as often as Madonna changed her hairstyle. No one worked harder to be the best-dressed and most informed member of each group. He became an encyclopedia of New Wave music in the fall, carried a briefcase in the winter and had the school believing he was a strung-out Rocker in the spring.

"Dude, I'm going to move into this one house where everyone is stoned all the time," he said to a crowd of seventh-graders at lunch one day, though I was certain he'd never even held a joint.

"Dude, that's so cool," a pizza-faced classmate said.

"How are you going to, like, get food?" I asked.

"Dude, when you're stoned, you don't even know when you're hungry."

Everyone nodded at this wisdom. Jake always had a way of capturing an audience, often using total bullshit.

In eighth grade, both of us landed jobs delivering newspapers for the *Seattle Times*. Jake had settled in to the Preps, striving to improve his social standing each day. So, we clung together as paper boy buddies in the evening, but Jake kept his distance at school by day as his status had surpassed mine. School Jake and Paper Boy Jake shared very limited common ground.

Despite our widening social-status gap, we spent more time together than any two people in the school. We devised a system of working our paper routes together to complete them faster. We took turns working each side of the street. To keep it interesting, we compared our "passing stats." If you chucked the paper and it landed on the porch, you completed the pass. He had the better arm, but I was more accurate. I'll never forget the day I went 41-for-41. The look of defeat on his face. Priceless.

All that time together led to conversations that went deeper than those typical of 8th graders. All those hours delivering the news. Countless more riding bikes to the store for a bottle of Jolt cola and a Clark bar. When I knew Jake back then, he was a briskly shaken bottle of Jolt. And, when I pried back his cap, his bad memories bubbled out of his mouth faster than he could suck them back in.

I believe this made Jake and I very close for a while, then led to him keeping his distance as we entered high school. He feared that I might unravel the canvas upon which he'd painted a picture of his suburban life for his fellow preps to see. Perfect Jake. His loving mother and step-father. Fictional tales of his father, which ranged from "He ate it in 'Nam" to "He tames lions for Barnum and Bailey, so he's on the road."

I knew the truth, and it was sad. Jake had been abused as a child. First by his father and then even worse by other men. Every type of abuse you could imagine, he once told me while we munched on Dunkin' Donuts after a Sunday morning *Times* delivery. His mother had done nothing to help him. He explained it away when he told me these stories–which I didn't believe at first. "She didn't know it was going on" one moment and "they would have killed her if she'd done anything" the next.

He seemed angrier at his father, but not just because of the abuse. He believed his father's departure invited even worse men into his life. He did not shed a tear when he told me these things, but his brown eyes seemed to darken.

I tried to shake off the memory and get back to the game. The A's broke a scoreless tie when the Mariners catcher blocked the plate to draw a catcher's interference call from the umpire. I hated the new rule, or any rule that seemed to soften a sport. I yelled at the TV, mostly to amuse myself, hoping the baseball commissioner and the umpire could hear me. "You fucking pussies are ruining my life," I said.

Old man Hanks, who'd dragged his yard-waste bin to the curb, scowled at me through the window I'd forgotten was open. That guy really hated me. He stared at my messy yard from his, which could be on a landscaping brochure. He was sure I was bringing down his property value.

He loved to yell at the neighborhood kids for being too loud, and he had a personal collection of Wiffle balls he'd confiscated. Just to screw with him, I bought dozens of Wiffle balls one day and dumped them out in my driveway for all the kids to see.

"Look at all these balls, kids," I said, loud enough for Old Man Hanks to hear. "Plenty of balls! We'll never run out!"

I'd like to say it was for the kids, but I was truly being nice out of spite. Maybe I am passive aggressive.

The Mariners manager argued with the umpire and got tossed. Instead of shouting at the TV some more, I let the Jake debate continue in my head.

8

I HEART KEITH MORRISON

Dateline NBC Facebook post: Trouble at Seneca Rocks: On Friday, Keith Morrison tells the story of the death of a small town's beloved mother of four.

Seneca Rocks? Huh. Only about an hour from where I lived for a few years as a kid.

A couple of weeks had passed since the Guadalupe incident. I had convinced myself that old Jake would never do such a thing. I was busy with work, coaching baseball and being a not-particularly exceptional father and husband, and I was not exactly Sherlock.

I set the DVR to record the episode.

I don't watch much TV, but I love Dateline for reasons I don't understand. Most episodes involve the death of a woman and the eventual conviction of her husband.

The husbands are idiots. They often try to set up a phony break-in. A robbery gone bad, except the robbers never take anything of real value. The husband has some thin alibi or none at all. Or there's the "oops-she-fell-down-the-stairs-golly-I-don't-know-why-there's-an-imprint-of-a-hammer-on-the-back-of-her-head" method.

Often the soon-to-be widower had found another woman who after months of fucking him decided he needed to leave his wife before they could continue their relationship. The husband then kills for one or more of the following additional reasons:

1. Insurance money: The best way to start a new life with your mistress is with a fat insurance check.
2. To keep his money: Figuring he's going to have to fork over half of everything, he decides he'd rather just keep it by ending his better half.
3. This one is my favorite: The guy with no money and no life insurance policy. He's just too gutless to break it off with the wife. He can't tell her, and he can't nut up and explain to his kids that he likes their new mommy better than the old one. In theory, it's a clean breakup, other than the carpet.

They all get busted and fall apart in the interrogation room. Turns out the cops aren't falling for the robbery. Golly, why was there still $68 in her wallet? Why was she still wearing her wedding ring? These dipshits can't explain these things and then try to fake-cry. She hasn't been found yet, but they talk about her in the past tense. Do these dumb fucks ever watch Dateline? Kathleen and I used to joke that we were taking notes so we wouldn't be so stupid.

Once in a while, there's a curveball. The husband gets thoroughly interrogated despite his alibi. For a moment, you think, "Oh, not the husband this time!" But, usually he's hired someone or convinced a new girlfriend that they'll all be happy if they could just get rid of the wife and save a few bucks. The hit man or mistress turns on him, and we find out that once again, it's the husband.

Always.

OK, about once every five years, there's a Dateline that ends with it not being the husband. He's usually harassed by the police, prosecutors and media for years before proving his innocence. After all, it's always the husband.

Almost always.

Kathleen loves to watch Dateline, too. I'm glad, because it might appear that I like all these dead wives a little too much without her watching with me. We don't miss an episode hosted by Keith Morrison. If Kathleen ever kills me, my only request is that Keith Morrison tells the story. Hell, I wish he'd read me a bedtime story.

Eight days after the Seneca Rocks episode aired, Kathleen and I finally watched it while eating freshly-delivered pizza.

Keith. Ahhhhh, Keith. After a long week, his voice felt like soaking in a hot tub. Tell me all about it, Keith...

"There's a reason John Denver sang about those West Virginia country roads. One might head down one of those old roads, and decide to stay awhile. Take the Buntley family for instance. A whimsical weekend turned into an annual visit, then a second home in, well, the place they belonged. But, ohhhhh, those country roads must end somewhere. On a particular glimmering late summer evening, the road came to a shocking end for this West Virginia mother of four, permanently darkening the country road to Seneca Rocks for all that had known her."

On his game tonight, Keith danced through the story like Fred Astaire. The rhythm. The way he hung on certain words. And the facial expressions. They often said more than the words. He broke out a special set of eyebrow movements for guilty husbands. Somehow, his brows said "I'm totally fascinated by everything you are saying" to the husband and "Do you see how this bum thinks I believe him?" to television viewers.

"Gee, ya think it's the husband?" Kathleen asked as her lips headed for her wine glass.

"Ya think?" I asked back, smiling at her. Before my smile faded, I took a liberal bite from my slice and chased it with a gulp of imperial stout.

Keith masterfully weaved the story. Wistful when he spoke to a choked-up teenage son. A wry smile when the brave 8-year-old girl reflected. I swear he was giving me a backrub, too.

Turns out Dianne Buntley had fallen from the top of Seneca Rocks. The Buntleys, enjoying a kid-free weekend (lucky bastards), decided to do the same thing many people have done at Seneca Rocks. Keep walking past the big STOP sign that also lists how many people had fallen to their deaths since 1971.

"Oh, but while the kids are away, the parents will play," said Keith, dressed in a leather jacket and jeans, gray hair flapping gently in the West Virginia breeze. If he were a 20-year-old hot girl, it could have been an '80s hair band video.

It was pretty obvious what had happened. Bill Buntley managed to farm off the kids for the weekend.

"Nice guy," I said. "Saved the kids from hearing the splat."

Kathleen's eyes moved partially toward mine, stopped and snapped back toward the television. Like when you call a dog and it pretends not to hear you after realizing there's no treat.

The Buntleys' relationship strained lately, Bill and Dianne thought a trip to the cabin might help them reconnect. What Dianne didn't know is that Bill was banging his coworker while hoping to take it to a more permanent level. The best way to do that was to have the wife fall down a few levels.

They walked through the Seneca Rocks stop sign and soon she "fell" to her death while attempting to get a better photo angle.

Keith, as usual, cast some doubt on Bill as the suspect. This is always part of the show. Without the glimmer of hope that it's not the husband this time, we might turn off the TV five minutes in. Keith told us how Bill had broken it off with the other woman months ago. He'd suffered a sprained ankle at some point during the hike, he said, and was unable to reach the top of the rocks. Did the injury occur before or after Dianne's death? And, Bill was one hell of an actor. We saw him cry, and there were tears. Usually these wife-killers can't manufacture those. They might bellow and shake, but those eyes are about as wet as my sister-in-law's overcooked Thanksgiving turkey.

Bill, just like every Dateline husband, looked like an idiot. He tried to explain he'd hurt his ankle close to the top of Seneca Rocks. He decided it wasn't worth it to go a few hundred more yards, but encouraged Dianne–never without a camera, according to Keith–to take a few photos while he rested for the trip down.

That alone might have been believable. But, Bill, apparently wanting to cement his innocence, claimed he saw a man wearing a mask or bandanna running into the woods shortly after hearing a scream. He stumbled to the ledge to find his wife had fallen. Or been pushed by this masked man. Gee, Bill, why not a one-armed man?

You almost had me on your side until you brought up that one. Nice try, Billy boy.

With viewers certain of Bill's guilt, Keith clouded suspicion once again. Normally I refused to walk down that path with Keith, though this one seemed different.

The ankle injury was legit, a photo of a black-and-blue ankle spun onto my TV screen as proof.

And, was there actually a masked man? Another hiker said he saw a guy wearing a similar getup to the one Bill described. No mask on the guy, but the rest, including approximate height and weight, seemed right, and the timing fit, too. There were some unexplained boot prints heading into the woods, but that was the case in several places along the popular hiking trail.

Yeah, right. Masked man. Boot prints.

Keith explained, "Bill was arrested at their Spruce Knob cabin…"

Wait a minute. Spruce Knob? That's a West Virginia high point! The one damned high point I'd been to in my life.

I chuckled. Not this again.

Jake?

Keith interviewed Bill. Tight zoom on Bill. Blue-collared shirt. That was never a good sign for the guy. I figured this interview took place at the state penitentiary.

I find it interesting when convicted murderers decide to talk to Dateline. Always awaiting a hopeless appeal, I imagined their lawyers hated Keith.

Idiots. Or narcissistic sociopaths. They are certain that viewers and potential jurors will buy their load of bullshit. It never works.

Except, Bill seemed different to me.

He explained the masked-man theory.

"So a masked man, rushes at her and throws her off the edge," Keith said, impassively.

Bill, crestfallen, admitted he probably wouldn't believe a story like this, either. He sounded shaky, likely from crying. His lips quivered as he spoke. He thoughtfully answered each question, though he appeared uncomfortable in front of the camera, not interested in putting on a show.

"Hmmm," I said, pausing the DVR with Bill's sad blue eyes, reddened from tear drops, staring toward Kathleen. "I don't know."

"You don't know what?" Kathleen asked, almost happy-go-lucky, kid-like.

"He just doesn't look like a killer to me. Don't think he has it in him."

"Judging by his wardrobe, the court didn't agree with you."

Yeah, I know. But, I don't know. Just look at his eyes. Do those look like the eyes of a killer?

"Let me look into your eyes," she said, mockingly.

I rolled my eyes, un-paused the DVR and watched Keith work his magic. As usual, he was perfect. The feigned wonder. The gritty smile when he liked Bill's answer, a quizzical head-tilt when he didn't. Bill hung in there, and you could see the worry. The deep concern that Keith didn't believe him, and the sigh of resignation that no one ever would.

"A masked man?" said Keith, with his eyebrows arched so high they nearly climbed above the silver hair combed perfectly away from his forehead. "Come ohhhnnn…"

Keith's wondrous smile quickly turned to a smirk that made Bill shrink. By now we knew that Bill was doing 25-to-life. There didn't seem to be enough evidence to nail him for Murder 1.

There was something about Bill. He either didn't do it, I thought, or had convinced himself of his own innocence. I found myself pulling for him. A guy who'd been convicted of murder by his peers, if 12 people who couldn't get out of jury duty were in fact his peers. I started to wonder why I felt badly for Bill before realizing that it was because my mind had wandered back to that high point, Spruce Knob.

I'd spent most of the first 9 years of my life in Parsons, West Virginia, about two hours away from Spruce Knob a relatively modest state high point at 4,683 feet. The highest point of the Allegheny Mountains could be reached by driving on some forest service roads and a short hike. Any 8-year-old could handle the hike, as I can easily attest.

Though Spruce Knob was the high point, Seneca Rocks was the bigger draw. Located about 20 miles north of Spruce Knob within the Eastern panhandle of West Virginia, Seneca Rocks served as a popular destination for rock climbers. I doubt any high-pointer ever went to Spruce Knob without making a stop at Seneca Rocks. Both hikes could easily be completed in an afternoon. No big deal for an 8-year old, and a walk in the park for a guy who runs marathons.

I noticed that my muscles had been flexing. I relaxed them, took a deep breath and slowly exhaled.

The voices in my head continued their fierce debate:

"Another mom, another mysterious death. He's a murderer."

"Stop being such a drama queen! What are the odds?"

"So, MILFs just happen to die everywhere this guy goes?"

"People die. They die all the time."

I wanted to kill my internal argument and my imagination. At this point I couldn't just ignore it, so I decided to simply find a way to rule it out. Quickly. You never want to know someone who's killing people, and I really didn't have the time or energy to deal with this crap.

What if there was something to this? This meant that not only was Jake a killer but this Bill guy's life had been ruined and ruined again. I tried to put myself in Bill's shit-covered shoes and shook off the thought. I wouldn't handle that well at all. First your wife dies. Then everyone despises you and as you get hauled away to meet Bubba in prison.

I dug my iPhone out of a pocket and picked some lint off the fingerprint-covered screen. In the hopes of ruling out Jake as a suspect, I decided to look at Jake's high point photos. All I needed was a different date than Dianne's fall.

On Jake's page, and then in his photos, I found the album labeled "High Points." There was his map of the United States, color-coded to show which high points he'd completed and the years he planned to complete the others. His future plans were organized by what appeared to be a combination of geographical symmetry and degree of difficulty. He'd pick off a few in the same region during a summer. Denali was a couple of years away, and then he'd bring it all back home by summiting Washington state's Mount Rainier.

He'd started slowly about five years ago, just picking off one or two a year. He probably worked them in as side trips during his countless excursions before making them primary destinations more recently.

Going to Mardi Gras? Why not summit Driskill Mountain–all of 535 feet? UW football game at Notre Dame? Take an extra day and pick off some Farm Belt high points! A little jealousy crept back in. Sounded fun. Except for the getting out of bed and hiking parts.

I glanced at the tiny photos on the screen, unable to tell them apart without clicking on each one individually and zooming in.

And, there it was. I felt my heart pounding in my chest.

Through a mild sunlit fog, trees with green leaves that would soon turn to spectacular shades of red, yellow and orange before falling to the ground, there it was. Jake, with four fingers in the air to signify his fourth high point. Proudly he stood with an arm around the sign held in place by logs sprouting from the ground:

Spruce Knob
Elevation 4,863 Ft
Highest Point In
West Virginia

Jake, as he often did with such photos, used a date stamp that caused the pizza to start crawling from my stomach.

August 22, 2014

Dianne died on August 20, 2014.

That was the moment I became sure of it.

Jake Mallory was a serial killer.

9

OFF THE MEDS

Dateline Facebook post: Did Bill's story cause you to doubt the prosecutor's case?

Keep in mind that I'd had months to spin and internally debate the New York and Texas murders and high points. It started with me just kind of amusing myself. Hey, wouldn't it be funny if that asshole was, like, a really big asshole? I built a case and tore it down many times. It was, after all, ridiculous. Right?

Even now, I tried desperately to clear Jake. Maybe it wasn't him. Jake had been everywhere. There is death everywhere. They had intersected three times. Big freakin' deal.

I don't believe in coincidences, I heard Harry Bosch say.

"Hello?" Kathleen said after Keith's voice trailed off to end Dateline. "Helloh-ohhhhh."

I snapped out of it. I'd barely noticed the last few minutes of the show, though I did see two of Bill's kids holding their grandmother's hand as they walked down a path. She was raising them now.

"What's your deal?" she asked. "Husband did it again. Shocker."

"I don't know, he didn't seem like a guy who would knock off his wife."

Kathleen squinted at me as if to search for a clue that my brain still functioned.

"Yeah, that's probably what they'll say about you," she said. "I'd suggest avoiding the 'masked man jumped out of the bushes' defense."

"Yeah," I half-chuckled. It was all the post-show analysis I could offer Kathleen at the moment.

I needed to run this by someone.

"OK, this is going to sound a little crazy," I said to my wife.

"Another shocker," she offered, along with a cheeky grin.

Yeah, this was going to go well. I paused before stupidly moving forward.

"So, you know that guy I went to high school with? Jake Mallory?

"The roasted pig guy from the UW game? Yeah, I remember."

"He was right near Seneca Rocks the day that woman died."

"Oh my God!" she exclaimed, bug-eyed. "You've done it! You've found the masked man!"

"Just listen a second…"

"Hey, next time you see Jake, see if he's got a mask tucked in his pocket."

I sighed. This wasn't going to go anywhere. This is how we often interacted. We gave each other shit like fraternity brothers.

"Does he wear hoodies? That's suspicious. If he's wearing a Purple hoodie at the next UW game, bring him in for questioning, Sipowicz.

I leaned my head against the back of my chair and looked up at the ceiling. Big mistake. Time to abort this plan. I laughed it off the best I could and grunted, "I just might have to wear a hoodie the next time you go for a jog."

I looked at her, annoyed, while pretending to be mock-annoyed. Even in a baggy UW sweatshirt, she was beautiful. People never shied away from asking how I'd landed her. Comments ranged anywhere from "Wow, you, uh, married well" to "So tell me, Bob, how did your wife lose her eyesight?" I just smiled, and hoped they all assumed I had something special in my pants.

As I considered my options for a conversation subject change, Kathleen's phone alerted her to a text message, saving me from further ridicule. I regretted broaching the subject, but knew it would be quickly forgotten. Used to my tangents, she knew I'd move on to something else soon enough.

One way that Kathleen was perfect for me was her ability to counter-balance my sometimes extreme emotions. She could do this with just a glance that somehow made me look at myself. Or by a few words, like "How's it goin' there, Skip?" when I maybe got a little too worked up during a Little League game. Or by walking away from me in either real or mock disgust. She knew exactly what buttons to push to bring me back toward normal. No one else could do this. Sometimes, it was like playing with an old Chinese finger trap. Pulling me in the obvious direction only made me pull harder in the other. She knew when to use finesse or metaphoric brute force. Or throw water on my burning wick.

I guess that's why I stopped talking to her about Jake. A mental patient deciding to stop taking his meds. Something stopped me from wanting her to bring me back to the center. She wouldn't do this by saying, "I think you're fucking Looney Tunes!" That would only make me dig deeper into Jake's world to prove I was right. No, she'd do something truly annoying like, I don't know, act supportive. I really hate it when she does that. I didn't want her to look at me, pathetically, and say, "Maybe you should look into it." That would only make me not look into it. I wanted to avoid wisecracks that would cause me to laugh at myself and the entire situation. Somehow she'd find a way to make me realize that I was being silly about Jake. I just couldn't have that, though looking back it would have made our lives a hell of a lot easier.

10

RICK AND DICK

The Corwins' house
Mill Creek, Washington

Rhonda Corwin Facebook post: Getting our house ready for our guest's too arrive! So many reason's to celebate life!

A week after the Seneca Rocks revelation, my least-favorite busybody, Rhonda, hosted a barbeque. Though teammates for select baseball, our sons played on different spring Little League teams. Her son's Red Sox had beaten my son's Diamondbacks the previous weekend to all but sew up the league championship. She didn't say it, but I'm sure that's what we were celebrating.

Bitch.

"They'll have a lot of beer," Kathleen offered.

"I need more than beer."

As it turned out, there was more than beer. The Corwins lived in Mill Creek, a small city that sprouted from a golf course 30 years ago. My family's house sits two miles outside the city limits in unincorporated Snohomish County. One of the golf-course dweller dads had come across some scotch that would cost me a summer school salary. But, Rick, Exhibit B of my Derivations of the name Richard theory, was in a sharing mood. Obscured by an abandoned backyard cedar and plastic play set, he poured the amber liquid for his son's coaches, a crew-cut ex-cop Dick and me. Yes, I sipped Scotch with Rick and Dick. Rick could never be Richard, Ricky or Rich. And Dick could only be Dick.

Rick was the type of guy that, when he started talking, you made every effort to create enough white noise in your head to drown him out. He threw out a lot of words, but they never seemed to add up to a whole lot.

We knew Rick was still trying to butter us up for more playing time for his kid, who just didn't seem to want it as much as his dad. I could usually evade the kissing of my ass, but that was some damned good scotch. He wore a suit that looked expensive but didn't fit quite right, like he got a great deal but they didn't carry his size. Rick, still clinging desperately to the dwindling hair on the top of his head, likely paid a lot for a hair stylist but was getting bad advice. Time to give up and cut it tight, Rick. It ain't growing back.

Dick was pretty much the opposite of Rick. He didn't say much, but when he did I ate up his words like they were chili fries in danger of going cold. He started coaching with me when his grandson joined our team.

Aside from his baseball knowledge, his personality was precisely what I needed in the dugout. Like my baseball version of Kathleen. I was the hothead in danger of going all Piniella on umpires at any moment. He was the one who put a hand on my shoulder–just enough for me to come back to Earth and avoid going viral on YouTube. I was tough on kids at times, but also their biggest cheerleader. Dick was, well, Dick, all the time. Calm. A giant crevasse could be opening up underneath and he'd calmly step to the side while motioning others to join him. He could win a Power Ball jackpot and accept the check like a grocery coupon for a free can of tuna. He'd served tours in Vietnam, and had certainly seen unspeakable things that would make me shrivel up like a nut sack in a glacial lake.

Recently, I'd considered talking to Dick about Mallory. I knew he would listen intently and it would make sense to get an old cop's opinion. I'd ruled it out, mostly because I didn't want to see that look on his face. The one that, without him ever needing to open his mouth, said, "I love you and I feel sorry about this, but you're not right this time."

After making a dent in the bottle, Rick gave up on us and went to work on someone else. The scotch had done its job, and the liquid inhibition-remover soaking in my synapses led to me running my theory by Dick after we switched to beer.

"OK," Dick said with his uneven but soothing voice, the kind you end up with when you used to yell a lot but had stopped long ago. "So your old high school buddy was around the scene of a crime that you saw on Dateline?"

The "saw on Dateline" part hurt a bit. Patronizing. We weren't off to a good start.

"Yeah, but there are two others," I said, overshadowed by Rick laughing too hard at someone's joke–likely his own–on the other side of the yard. "There was the one in New York, and the one in Texas."

"And those women have never been found," he said, more of a statement than a question. I read between those words–the West Virginia crime was much different than the other two and I was trying to link them together.

"Well, yeah, but he's going to heavily forested areas. Lots of places to hide somebody. Maybe the West Virginia one was more of an impulse. He liked it, but decided to be more careful with the others. The high points are, I don't know, like his trophies."

"Trophies. Huh, yeah," said Dick with a kind, almost sympathetic look as he organized his words carefully. Shit. That look on his face–the one I feared–was forming. He sucked in the left corner of his mouth as he considered his approach. It reminded me of his face when one of our pitchers struggled. He knew the kid needed to be pulled off the mound despite the potential psychological ramifications associated with failure. You can either pull him or leave him in and hope he works through it.

"New York and Texas," he said, pausing and showing a wince of hope that I'd come to his conclusion before he had to state it. I didn't, so he continued, "Lot of people in those places."

"Yeah, I know, but isn't that too much of a coincidence?" I said weakly, like a defensive jab from a boxer who's about one right hook away from landing on the canvas. "Throw in that he had kind of a rough childhood. Doesn't that add up to something?"

I said the last part like a little kid at the vet's office, asking hopefully if there's anything else the vet can do to save Sparky before they put down the old dog.

Dick looked me in the eye, knowing he should give it to me straight without making me feel like a dipshit. I could see he felt sorry for me. He could sense that I really believed my theory, and it was uncomfortable for him to tell me I was deep in left field on this one. But, he also knew it had to be done. Like putting down old Sparky. Better to give it to me between the eyes than allow me any more suffering.

He opened his mouth to put me out of my misery.

"Hello again, boys!" slurred Rick, who'd apparently continued to sample the scotch while attempting to make deals with everyone in the yard. "Boy, that sssstuff will ssshhhoot right through ya! I thhhink I better hit the hhhhead."

I thought to myself, "Take my sorry-ass theory to the shitter with you."

11

THE WORST KIND OF ADDICT

Kathleen Facebook post: The kids just found the milk in the cupboard and the cereal in the fridge. I think Bob's brain is ready for summer break!

Like.

There's no doubt that I stumbled down the stretch of the school year. The finish line was in sight, and I wasn't exactly striving for Teacher of the Year.

I'd assigned research projects, mostly to work on my own research while coasting through the final two weeks. If only the students knew I was barely going to look at any of those projects. A quick glance to see that something was there, and a score that was just enough to bring up a grade a little bit. Just enough to stop the bitching and get me out of there the second my contract said I could leave for the summer.

I had been a horrible teacher that spring. I wasn't much of a youth baseball coach, father or husband, either. Undeterred by Dick, I'd spent too much time reading about death, and nearly every spare moment thinking about it.

I'd learned that Jake loved to travel in the good ol' U.S. of A. I had to admit, I admired that part. I, of course, was too financially challenged to travel anywhere other than the occasional weekend baseball tournament or to biennial family vacations to semi-attractive destinations.

Most people I know fall into four traveler categories:

- No-go: These people never go anywhere. They either can't afford it, or believe money is better spent in other ways. Why blow $10,000 on a vacation? That can buy one sweet used Camaro!
- Weekenders: This group likes quickies. Weekend for the kids at the hotel with the water park, romantic weekend in the San Juan Islands, wine destinations in Washington and California. These trips are reasonably-priced, but they don't work for me. I need a day to settle in, and by then the trip is half-over. And the last day is depressing, because the trip is almost at its end. That leaves about two hours on Saturday night to enjoy.
- Tropical vacations: As David Lee Roth once sang, "I got a drink in my hand, I got my toes in the sand." There's not much else to those vacations, and that would be just fine with me.
- World travelers: London, Vienna, Paris, Southern Italy. African Safari in a Land Rover. OMG, the smog is so bad in Beijing! Might as well be the Red Planet as far as I'm concerned. I wasn't going to these places any time soon. Just thinking about it was exhausting.

What amazes me about world travelers is that some of them have never seen North America. (Layovers on the way to Europe don't count.) No Yellowstone. No Grand Canyon. No Disney World. No Niagara Falls. It is all, I suppose, beneath them. So, they fly over all of these wonders, crisscrossing Europeans who ironically are completely blown away by Old Faithful. Apparently the grass is always greener on the other side of the ocean. To me, it's like circumventing 10 hot girls in your neighborhood to get to the bitchy one on the other side of town. I'm not saying the bitchy girl doesn't offer some benefits. I'd just check on the ones in the neighborhood first.

Jake seemingly took every minute of every weekend and vacation week to see what his country had to offer. He'd been to every legendary sports venue. He'd fly-fished in Montana and hunted alligators in Mississippi.

I loved road trips and envied his spare time and spare money. He lived and breathed the United States of America and displayed it proudly on Facebook.

One Facebook photo album showed the counties–not states, counties–he had visited. Nearly half of the 3,000-plus counties in the U.S. Another album, labeled "Jake's Blue Highways" showed wacky photos he'd taken during his travels. None of these were typical tourist photos. A car on top of a telephone pole in South Carolina. The Beaverlick Trading Post and Big Bone Lick State Park, just a few miles apart in Kentucky.

By now, I'd used Facebook to map out everywhere Jake had checked-in or taken a selfie for the past 5 years. All while ignoring my students during class time. I'd space out and think about it while forgetting to give the steal sign to a baserunner or while half-listening to my daughter's voice recital.

I looked and felt like shit–even by my low standard of existence.

"Are you OK?" Kathleen asked me that June, when I completely failed to hear anything she'd said at the dinner table.

"I'm sorry, just a lot going on."

"There's always a lot going on."

"I know, just tired I guess. I'll rally. The school year's almost over."

She looked at me, concerned, sensing there was more to it but didn't push the issue. She got up from the table, plates in one hand while touching my shoulder with the other. I liked that. A loving gesture not polluted by words.

While researching Jake, I attempted to cross-reference his trips with deaths or missing moms. There were several possibilities. Tammy Weaver, another award-winning mommy disappeared from Little Rock, Arkansas a couple of days before Jake hiked Magazine Mountain.

I guessed that Jake was either not killing all that often, or that he was being more careful. He was not foolish enough to grab a girl in the town next to the mountain and then bury her there. If he was indeed killing women, he was choosing them carefully in towns a few hours away from his high point. Sometimes maybe even from a neighboring state. Based on my research he'd killed dozens of women. Or maybe no women. As much as I'd spun my wheels, I hadn't gone very far.

Of course there were missing women everywhere. Just like the police and media, I ignored anything that didn't involve a mom from a wholesome, middle-class family. For all I knew, Jake had killed hitchhikers, hookers or his own mother. But, what could I prove? He'd made a very public display of his travels, and I assumed used stealth mode when he killed. There would be no gassing up in the victim's town. No video of him at Wal-Mart buying a shovel, tarp and rope. Too smart for any of that.

Aside from Seneca Rocks, it seemed like none of these women were ever found. If they were, it sure appeared like the husband was guilty. But, then again so was the Seneca Rocks guy, at least according to police. I thought about that poor bastard. Dead wife, hated by his own kids and society. Probably getting ass-raped in prison. I shivered at the thought that there might be more guys like

Bill out there. I couldn't think of too many things worse than being falsely convicted of killing your own wife. They'd find me hanging by my belt in a courthouse bathroom.

Although I wasn't in that situation, all of my time and effort had done nothing but endanger my job and marriage. I had nothing but my gut. I had nothing that would convince the police, Dick or even my own wife. Hell, at times I couldn't even convince myself.

I'd played through taking my high points theory to a police station. *So, guys, here's a list of all the high points my buddy's summited. And, here are all the dead women. Can you go arrest him now? Golly gee, thanks guys!*

Oh, you have a few questions?

No, officer, none of them were from a town right by the high point.

No, none of the women missing, hundreds of miles from the high points, have ever been found.

No, I've never seen him kill anyone.

No, he's not the only high-pointer in America, and no, I don't think they are all murderers.

No, I don't have a damned thing that's worth even a second of your time.

I pictured myself walking out of the police station, and the cops all erupting in laughter just a split second before the door closed behind me. I know it sounds pathetic, but that more than anything else stopped me from talking to anyone about this. I didn't want to look like a fool. I probably was a fool, I thought.

Finally, the school year ended. It was always like a heavyweight fight to me. Those last few rounds, I always staggered along, just trying to keep upright and hope I'd win a decision. Now that the final bell mercifully had rung,

I could do yard work to keep Old Man Hanks off my back, and I could stop ignoring my own family.

Or I could try to figure out what the hell Jake was going to do next.

Every day, I decided to forget the whole thing. I was probably crazy, and no one was going to listen to me anyway. And, what the hell was I going to do? Buy a Great Dane and a van and solve a mystery? I can hear Jake now, mask removed like at the end of a Scooby Doo cartoon: "I would've gotten away with it, too, if it hadn't been for that meddling, middle-aged fat guy."

But, something stopped me from throwing in the towel. I couldn't forget those dead women. And, of more immediate concern, the next dead mother. Sometimes drug addicts get sober. Serial killers had a harder time with their addictions.

During the moments I tried to convince myself I was nuts, I leaned on the following hopes:

1. There was no serial killer: I was just being silly. People die and people climb mountains. They don't have to be connected. Perhaps I could look at the calendar of any high pointer and connect them to women disappearing.
2. There were no dead women! Maybe these women I'd researched had simply run off with another man, leaving behind beautiful children and loving husbands without a trace.
3. The cops would catch Jake any day now. Maybe they were closing in on him. What did they need from me? Nothing! I had nothing to offer anyone. So, sit back, drink a beer and let the pros do their jobs.
4. Jake was a killer, but he was all better now! Maybe Jake would take a look in the mirror one

day, and think, "Golly, Jake. Maybe killing mommies isn't such a great idea after all! He'd go get some help and find another hobby, like porn or something.

No. 2 was just stupid, and I always ruled out No. 4. He wouldn't stop. He would get caught or die. I'd read about serial killers a bit while blowing off my life. They lacked empathy, so there would be no concern for the families of dead women. Serial killers usually got better at it, honing their craft with each kill. Quite often, they quickened the pace. How many would Jake kill this summer? I may be frozen in place by suburban life, but the ice was melting and Jake would be high-pointing again. Which kids would lose a mother this summer? (And probably see their dad get dragged away to jail.)

Three things, I decided. Talk to Jake. Follow him on his next trip, hopefully without being noticed. Don't grow the nads to mention any of this to anyone, because I'd just look like an idiot. No one would believe me anyway.

12

Our No. 1 Fan

Federal Way, Washington

My Facebook message to Mallory: Hey, Jake! I'm going to be in town this weekend, and thought maybe we could grab a beer. You around?

I hit send and my heart rate quickened. What the hell was I doing? I wondered what Jake would think when he saw the message. It was out of character for me. I hadn't "grabbed a beer" with someone from high school since drinking underage in the Hoagie's Corner parking lot, trying desperately to fit in.

While I didn't believe Jake would think I was trying to figure out if he was a murderer, he had to wonder what was up. For a moment I thought about pretending to be an Amway salesman. Or maybe a cult member. That was more believable than, "just wanted to catch up and grab a beer!"

My mind raced for only a few minutes before Jake replied, "Yeah, Dawg! Let's do it! What's the occasion?"

"Nothing special. Just in town for a baseball tournament and thought it'd be fun."

"Sweet, dude! Where and When?

On a subconscious level, I must have assumed he'd say no, because his answer caused my pulse to quicken.

So, this was really going to happen? He wasn't too busy? Wasn't there a mountain to climb, a porno movie to reenact?

"We've got a game at 3 p.m., so maybe right after that."

"Cool! How about if I come check out the game and we go from there?"

I hesitated. Probably too long. I didn't like this at all.

"Yeah, that works."

I regretted hitting send but didn't see a way out. This is fucking great. I could see it now: "Hey, serial killer buddy! Meet my kids. And here's my wife–bet you'd like to kill her, huh? Why, she's just your type!"

The baseball tournament was set in Federal Way, where I'd lived after moving from West Virginia. It was one town over from Des Moines, my home when I met Jake in seventh grade. Not Des Moines, Iowa. Des Moines, Washington, where we pronounce the second "s" just so you know we're different.

It was only 50 miles away from my house but downtown Seattle separated my childhood home from my current home. Not being a fan of traffic I made every possible excuse to avoid the trip, which could turn into three hours if you tried it at the wrong time.

Jake showed up a half-hour early for the game. Just like in high school, Jake was all-in.

He wore our team colors–an easy one because it was purple like our beloved Huskies. He'd found out that our name was Diamond Dawgs (a name I hated, but inherited when I took over the team after parents figured out the previous coach had been stealing team funds), and had carefully written the word Diamond on a piece of paper and taped it above "Dawgs" on a shirt he undoubtedly already owned. He wrote it like when an adult tries to imitate a kid's handwriting. Organized sloppiness.

And cleats. The dude wore cleats. I was sure he had listened to John Fogerty's "Centerfield" on the way to the game. He was ready to play today.

He became our biggest fan, though he sounded like someone from the 1940s. This was a select team, not a Little League team, so he actually didn't sound totally out of place.

"Hey, you gotta wear that," he yelled when a 10-year-old ducked to avoid being hit by a pitch. "Rub some dirt on it," he hollered when another kid was a little slow to get up after diving for a ball. Moms chuckled. It was fun for those not wondering if he was going to kill them.

When our opponent, the Raptors, took the field on defense, Jake asked their third baseman if he was aware that dinosaurs were extinct. When my son walked near the fence, he congratulated him for overcoming his gene pool. He occasionally mixed in play-by-play that sounded like Keith Jackson calling the Rose Bowl.

"Whoa, Nelly, it's a fumbllllllle," he said when the other team made an error.

"The looooneliest man on a baseball field is the one standing behind the catcher, wearing a mask," he said after parents razzed the umpire for calling a high pitch for strike three to end an inning. At that moment I wished he'd lay off the moms and start taking out umps who call strikes on pitches above the letters.

He became the life of the stands, though no one was quite sure what to make of him. I overheard just enough of this to recall the off-kilter charm that drew people to Jake. It's why people wanted to hang out with him back in high school. It's why some part of me still wanted him to think of me as a friend, and why I remained bitter that he'd social-climbed well above me in high school. Yeah, I know. Pathetic.

Why would such a man need to kill? He was different than many serial killers. More like a Ted Bundy. A public golden-boy shell covering a private, black hole of a man.

The game ended in dramatic fashion, with my son hitting a ball to shallow right-center. Timmy (son of the annoying Facebook mom who wasn't quite annoying enough for me to justify kicking him off the team) was at second base when my son hit the ball, and he hesitated before finally taking off.

As he approached third, I saw the fielder bobble the ball as it skipped on the uneven grass. I jumped up and down and waved Timmy in, almost keeping up with him down the base line. The outfielder recovered and fired to the catcher, who put the tag down. I slumped. Everyone in the ballpark saw he was out, but the "loneliest man on the baseball field," after a momentary hesitation, spread his arms out and yelled, "Safe!" Extra-loudly, the way umpires do when they're not sure and want to sell it.

As the Diamond Dawgs sprinted out of the dugout to tackle Timmy at home plate, the Raptors completely lost their minds as the dust swarmed around backstop. Jake waved goodbye to them, which certainly didn't help. The ump had blown several calls during the game, and owed us one, but the other side didn't believe in the theory that it all evens out in the end.

The Raptors threw gloves against the fence. Bats and balls tumbled in the dugout. The team manager sprinted out of the dugout, gesturing at the plate and reenacting the play as the umpire began looking for the exit. Raptors moms and dads screamed at him.

"He was out by a mile!"

"You need to get some glasses, blue!"

"How much did they pay you?"

"You suck!"

The umpire, in his sixties I guessed, simply smiled and sauntered away. He'd likely made his fair share of shitty calls and heard all of it before. My skin could never be that thick. I gathered the Diamond Dawgs together and started the "2-4-6-8, who do we appreciate" thing. The Raptors, however, felt unappreciated, avoiding the post-game high fives for a quick exit and group pout session.

With all the fallout and a quick postgame team meeting, I had completely forgotten about my planned meeting with Jake. Yeah, that's how wrapped up I get in little kid baseball. I lose track of the serial killer cheering for them. I stood with my family as he strolled confidently toward us, sunglasses protecting me from those dark eyes. I forced a smile. It'd been a long day and grabbing a beer with a murderer sounded as appealing as cleaning the carpet after the dog pukes up the remains of a tennis ball.

"Helluva game! Kid was safe all the way," he said, winking at my son, who smiled at his new favorite person. I felt sudden horror for introducing my family to a killer.

"Yeah, that was a close one," I said. "Well, you ready?"

I was already stepping away from my family, wanting to put distance between them and Jake as quickly as possible.

"Yeah…," he trailed off just before a light bulb seemingly appeared over his head and a look of kid-on-Christmas took over his face. "Hey, how about we all go out!"

"Yes!!" screeched my son, who wasn't the first to fall for Jake's charm.

"I don't know…," I said, searching for an excuse, knowing I'd never overcome his instant grip on my family.

My wife, head tilted to the side and eyebrows raised, looked at me with resignation.

"Come on, Dad!" chirped Annie, an 8-year-old who always thought everything sounded like the best thing ever, psychopaths included.

"Come on, Dad!" chirped Jake, playing the role of my third child.

I recalled an episode of the television show *Friends*. The one where Chandler lies to a girlfriend that he's been relocated to Yemen to escape the relationship. He figures they would say their goodbyes at his apartment and he'd quickly be forgotten. She decides to see him off at the gate and watch the plane depart, unintentionally calling his bluff. "Well, then, I guess I'm going to Yemen!"

Me too, Chandler. Me, too. I guess I'm going to dinner with a serial killer.

At a chicken-wing chain restaurant, we ate mediocre food and drank good beer surrounded by large flat-screen TVs and music that was a bit too loud. We mostly talked about Jake's favorite subject: Jake.

We reminisced a bit. Jake told a great story about the time a group of people that included Jake and me played a practical joke on the cheerleaders.

"They didn't have cell phones back then, kids," Jake said, channeling Ward Cleaver before the big finish. "So, guess who had to go home with no pants!"

I didn't have the heart to tell him that I wasn't actually there, and invitations to stupidity like that were rare for me in high school. Moments like that, I'm thankful for beer.

"Look, I've got to ask," Jake said.

Kathleen and I both looked back at him, blankly. The kids, bored by old people talk, had started playing with some sort of computerized trivia game on the table.

"Yeah?" I asked, waiting for him to get to the point.

"Did you lose a bet or something?" he said, eyes fixed on Kathleen, hands gesturing toward me. "A foreigner looking for citizenship? Wake up with amnesia and he claimed to be your husband?"

Kathleen laughed, awkwardly. I smirked and nodded.

"How you landed this, I'll never know," he said, after his hands and eyes traded targets. "You've done all right, Peddin."

"Gee, thanks Jake," I said, mockingly. "I think you've done all right, too."

Kathleen looked at her wrist. There was no watch there, but it was still the international signal for, "We've been here long enough, and you need to get us out of here."

Jake caught her, and said, "Oh, yeah, you don't want to hear us ramble."

"Well, a few kids from the team are coming over to swim at the lake, so we really should get over there."

"Oh, wait," Jake said, eyes shifting to me. "Are you staying at your grandparent's place on the lake?"

The house, on little Steel Lake, was now inhabited by my mom and her husband. Jake had been there once or twice when we were kids. Kathleen, the kids and I were all staying there during the tournament weekend.

"Bob, why don't you invite Jake?"

I wanted to barf. Great plan. Introduce a serial killer to my wife, kids and mother all in one day. But, I also knew that maybe this would be a chance to see if I could get anything out of Jake, hopefully without sacrificing any family members.

So, out the door we went. One happy family and a serial killer. My wife typed away on her phone, and before

I knew it there were kids swimming and parents knocking back drinks at my mom's house.

Evenings like this were why we all loved June baseball. The kids cannonballed off the dock and drifted on yellow rafts. Parents sat on the patio, laughing and drinking. Really, the baseball games served as a preamble to the party.

My mom, still a hippie at heart, broke out a bottle of tequila and encouraged parents to take shots. Retired now, I envied her energy and youthful spirit. Sometimes I felt older than her.

I'd been sitting with Jake, reminiscing and talking UW football. With some big-time recruits, we hoped the team would get back to the glory days of our youth. We criticized the uniforms worn by college teams.

"I remember when you could turn on the TV and know who was playing just by looking at the uniform," Jake said. "Now, everyone's wearing gray. Or chrome, with a different uniform every week."

"Maybe they should think more about learning how to tackle than their freaking hairdos and uniforms," I muttered, eyes rolling.

My mom walked Kathleen over to us like she was a child that had been playing in the street and demanded that we take a shot together.

"A family that drinks tequila together, stays together," Mom said.

Jake looked at me and smiled, eyes saying, "Your mom is a little different than I remember."

I remembered then that my mother, who seemed to like everyone, never quite approved of Jake. She didn't flat out say it, but her mouth always turned downward when I mentioned his name. Maybe mother does know best, though it was hard to decide that definitively as my mom passed out shot glasses and started pouring.

With a couple of drink in her already, I wasn't so sure about Kathleen taking a shot. She rarely drank, and was a total lightweight. Like most people, the filter failed when she got lathered up.

With my mom supervising, I handed Jake and Kathleen a lime wedge and kept one for myself. We all looked at each other, anticipating the shot like sprinters in starting blocks. Jake raised his eyebrows, and lifted the shot glass above his head as if it were the starter's pistol. We tilted back our heads and the glasses and took a hard swallow. We bit into our lime wedges, letting the sour liquid mask some of the tequila's burn. We all gasped, coming up for air.

Jake took the post-shot lime out of his mouth and continued his story about his trip to West Virginia. I'd brought up the state with a tasteless joke about my early education and led him into a conversation about his trip. Getting Jake to talk about himself was not a difficult task.

Jake, of course, had fully immersed himself in West Virginia culture during his three days in the state. He'd eaten pepperoni rolls and sucked down pickled ramps, a wild leek that I had dug in the hills when I was a kid. He even knew the background behind the phrase "Mountaineers are always free." Shit, he knew more about West Virginia than most of its residents. Impressive as always, and for a moment I forgot about my half-witted theory. It seemed ridiculous, right? Serial killers are supposed to be that guy who never quite fits in. Quiet. A little creepy. The guy you don't really notice. Undoubtedly Jake seemed different than the rest of us, but not serial-killer different.

I began dismissing my theory, in part because it wasn't any fun to think about it. I had a nice buzz going, and why blow it with death?

Kathleen, however, unintentionally reminded me of why I was here, and also why I should never have mentioned my theory to her. She listened to Jake, then slowly turned her eyes toward me and slurred, "What else do you do on those trips? You didn't happen to push anyone off a rock while you were there, did you?"

Suddenly sober, my pulse quickened and whatever muscles I had left tensed.

Kathleen laughed a little too loudly, the way you do when you're buzzed. Sure, Jake's funny when he's not killing people, my love. Jake's eyes widened slightly, but he recovered quickly. Almost quickly enough for me not to see it. It lasted less than a second, but it seemed clear he knew what Kathleen was referencing.

"Huh?" he said.

"Oh, we watched this episode of Dateline," she continued. "Bob had seen your high-point stuff on Facebook and pointed the finger at you. But, the husband did it. It's always the husband," she said, glazed eyes peering into mine.

Jake was quick, but I could see his mind racing for a beat. He decided to acknowledge that he knew about the story. He often posted on Facebook about current events, and pretending to have missed that story would not have fit. His mind raced along with my pulse.

"Yeah, I heard about that," he said. "Seneca Rocks, right?"

Jake's dark eyes cut into mine. He opened them up, trying to read me. What did I know? Were we just messing around, or did I actually think there was something to this? My skin hurt.

I tried to recover the best I could.

"Yeah. I was pretty interested in that one because I'd been there. And Spruce Knob. Hey, only 49 more high points for me to go, right?"

I smiled weakly. Funny, huh Jake?

He looked into my eyes again. "Yep, it's always the husband."

13

WHISKEY AND STEEP STAIRS

Kathleen facebook post: No more shots for me! Ever!

The next day, with hungover coaches, the Diamond Dawgs finished second in the tournament to the Cubs and their damned cowbell. I most certainly did *not* need more cowbell. No one should ever have a cowbell at a baseball game. The only acceptable places for a cowbell are in a room with Christopher Walken or on a cow. With my head pounding from the night before, I thought a lot about all the places I could shove that cowbell.

Jake had excused himself the night before, not long after the Seneca Rocks conversation. I thought about him going home, and realized I didn't know exactly where he lived. Based on some Facebook posts, I assumed he still lived in our high school town.

After the party died down, I spent much of the night in and out of sleep, wondering what I knew. And what Jake thought I knew. And what he might do with what he thought I knew. And what I should do with what I thought I knew. He'd met my family now, and it would take no time at all for him to find our address. I decided to just hope he figured that, just like in high school, I was insignificant. That was my biggest asset: Nothingness.

Home on Sunday evening after the tournament, I flipped on SportsCenter–a sure way to keep Kathleen out of the family room–and sipped on a little hair of the dog.

I went to Jake's profile and found and album called "home sweet home."

Apparently, he'd inherited his mom's house. It looked the same, a late-60s tri-level, painted brown with white trim. His yard was impeccable. Various shrubs and trees that I couldn't begin to identify, manicured perfectly, decorated the property. Old Man Hanks would love this guy. One shrubbery photo featured the caption, "Just in case you were wondering, I like it trimmed short, not clean shaven."

Did all killers have nice yards?

"No sign of fresh graves," I muttered to my nearly naked ice cubes.

Gone was the old mauve carpet, replaced by shining hardwoods. He labeled the photo, "having fun with my hard wood."

I could see the staircase in one photo. I remembered it well. It led to the bottom floor, which was where we hung out on occasion. The staircase was steeper than most, and you had to really watch your step if you didn't want to end up in a heap at the bottom. I recalled that Jake had once explained that the builder elected to allow more open area on the low level rather than have it taken up by the staircase. Great, plenty of room to land when someone falls on their face. Why he hadn't labeled the staircase photo "going down hard and fast," I wasn't sure.

A shot of the kitchen made me think of Jake's mom. Always a cigarette in her hand. Just striking enough that you couldn't help but give her a quick onceover when you walked in the door. Big, big blond hair that was normal in 1985 but only worn by crazy people these days.

I couldn't recall ever speaking with her. All adults might as well have been semi-friendly aliens to me back then. Willing to coexist, but wary of each other's presence.

We spoke the same language, but our dialects differed greatly. I took circular routes around parents back then in an effort to avoid having to pretend to be polite.

I didn't think it back then, but now I pictured her with sad eyes surrounded by a wrinkled forehead. As a kid, all mothers seemed ancient to me, but I do think she was fairly young. Low, but hard miles.

I recalled awkwardly asking Jake about her last fall. "A moment of silence for Jake's mom," I said before rattling ice cubes as I drained the last few drops from my glass.

Jake's mom. Dead. Accident.

A terrible thought crossed my mind.

I dumped the ice cubes for some younger, perkier ones and splashed them with more Irish whiskey.

I picked up my phone to do some research about Jake's mom. I quickly realized this wasn't going to be easy. I knew she had married at least once after Jake was born, and that there'd been a few men in her life. I hadn't the slightest clue about her last name. I wasn't even certain of her first name. Sherry? Sharon? Cheryl?

Fuck. How could I forget this kind of stuff? I made a mental note to teach my kids to not be such self-centered pricks. To actually look adults in the eye and engage in conversation and not go through life with their heads up their asses (or heads up their phones). My evolutionary gift to them.

I put down my phone and grabbed the work laptop I hadn't checked back in on the last day of school as my principal instructed.

I Googled "obituary, accident, des moines." *Wow, people sure do die a lot*, I thought.

"Obituary, accident, stairs, des moines." A former Olympic swimmer had taken her first steps since a terrible accident. Fascinating. I almost read the story from the newspaper in Des Moines, Iowa, shaking my head and getting back to my task.

Just like everything I tried when it came to Jake, this was going nowhere.

Then, I thought about him. He'd want an obituary in the newspaper. Jake loved newspapers. Even back in our newsboy days, I could see he liked them. He also had a Facebook photo album called "in the news," which featured news and sport pages he viewed as significant. Like me, he'd clutched an actual printed copy of a newspaper in his hand every morning. It was just a matter of what died first–him or the newspaper business.

Jake would want his mother's obituary printed in the *Seattle Times*. He would want people to see it, and he would keep multiple copies for himself. I checked his Facebook page but came up empty. All sports and major news stories. No personal stuff.

What was her damned name? It wasn't going to come to me. It wasn't just my poor memory–I didn't give a shit 25 years ago and probably never knew her last name.

I went to the *Times* website, and searched for "obituary, accident, des moines."

Still a lot of dead people.

"Obituary, accident, des moines, Sherry." One dead Sherry, and a few named Sherry in the "survived by" paragraph.

"Obituary, accident, des moines, Sharon."

I'll be damned. Hello, Sharon. I read the obit.

Sharon Horton died July 13, 2008 in a tragic accident inside her Des Moines home, a place she loved. She was 47.

Sharon, a life-long Seattle-area resident, attended Roosevelt High School prior to a career in the banking industry.

I skimmed down to the bottom while thinking I hoped someone would make me sound interesting in my obituary.

Sharon is survived by her son Jake Mallory…

No other sons or daughters mentioned. A sister and nephews who lived in Montana. She loved to work in her yard, etc. There was no description of the accident. I thought about those stairs and shuddered.

I did a quick search for Sharon Horton death, and found only the obituary for multiple women with the same name. No article about investigations. I then realized that it didn't really matter. He may have killed her, pushed her down those steep stairs. Or maybe she just fell. She could be at the top of his list of death, but I couldn't do anything for her or any of the others already on the list. I think that's when it sunk in that every day I sat on my ass was another day that a woman might die. "He could be killing someone right now while I'm fucking around with Google," I whispered to the last few drops of whiskey in my glass. Each death from here forward, would be my fault. The weight of that increased the strength of my headache.

I wanted desperately to keep the list from growing, but had no idea how to prevent it.

I sunk in my chair and tipped back my glass. The ice cubes tried to break free but my colander teeth kept them where they belonged.

14

THE MAN WHO KNEW TOO MUCH

Rhonda Corwin Facebook post: Happy Fathers Day to all u Dad's out their. Especially to my man, you're the greatest Daddy in the world.

I "liked" the post even though I didn't like it. Ah, Father's Day. The day where middle-aged men make that awkward call to their dads. I had a distant relationship with my father, in part because we lived on opposite coasts for most of my life.

My parents divorced when I was 6 years old. I didn't remember the divorce very well. It seemed odd that they were sleeping in separate rooms in our old house on what was known as Quality Hill in Parsons, West Virginia. The only other memory of the divorce was watching my dad pull away with an old recliner resting in the back of his late '50s Chevy step-side truck.

A couple of years later, my mom had seen enough of those country roads and moved us back home to Seattle. I saw my dad sparingly after that. A few summers here and there. A couple of Christmases. A weekly phone call, but only for a few minutes and only after 8:00 p.m. *The long distance company charged an arm and a leg during daylight hours, you know.*

It wasn't perfect, but I couldn't complain to someone like Jake. His father had also left at around age six, but there was no recliner in the back of the squad car.

I'd never met John Mallory, Jake's father. I'd wondered why Jake had kept his name instead of using his mother's. It seemed like a daily reminder of the horrors he'd seen as a kid.

Memory of my last days of married parents is fuzzy perhaps because it was anti-climactic. Like the end of a good long piss. A couple of secondary streams, a couple of shakes and it's done. Jake's memory, however, seemed clear as the vodka I'd switched to earlier after running out of Jameson.

Jake had told me plenty during our paper route days. It was not a terribly original story. John like to drink, and when he drank, he liked to pound his wife. If she wasn't available, he moved on to his son.

Jakes stories captivated me. I'm not sure why he told me. I guess he wanted the release, and I was just one of those guys. People tell me things, even though I don't want to hear them most of the time. I'm not interested, but I'm good at feigning interest. Also, I have a face that, though not overly attractive, seems to draw people. Babies love me. According to one of Kathleen's friends it's because I look like a giant baby. I'm the guy comedians like to mess with during their act, and back before everyone had cell phones I was the one everyone asked for the time. I didn't hate it, but I didn't like it either. It just seems misleading, my face.

Jake said his dad didn't beat him as often as his mother, but once smacked him across the kitchen when Jake had dropped a glass. He'd landed in the broken glass, which cut into his legs and fingers while a purple bump formed on his cheek.

Another time, when the screams from a drunken argument had subsided, Jake walked into his parents' room. He was hungry. Mom had been too busy with knuckle sandwiches to make him something to eat. He opened the door, and saw his father on top of his mother. He could see rage in his eyes as he moved up and down on his mother with his hands around her throat. He thought it was horrible that they were fighting. I didn't have the heart to tell him it was worse than he realized.

Jake quickly exited the room, but didn't get far. After some commotion and a few shouts, he heard footsteps pounding down the hallway, echoed by his own heartbeats. He hid behind a couch as the footsteps grew angrier, head buried between his hands and knees. Spotted, he soon felt the sting of a hand on his backside.

"What the fuck do you think you're doing?"

The voice stunned him more than the physical violence. He looked up just in time to see his mother's hand closing in on his face.

"Don't you *ever* come in there again without knocking! Do you hear me?"

When Jake told me this story, he said it hadn't been his mom's fault. She'd been the victim. But, I remember his eyes had looked empty when he said that. It was like a quarterback saying it wasn't the receiver's fault the pass was dropped in the end zone. It was just something you say because it sounds right, even if no one, including you, believes it.

A few months after that incident, cops hauled away John Mallory. Jake wasn't sure why, but believed it may have had something to do with writing bad checks or embezzlement or both. His last memory of his father was seeing him in handcuffs, head pushed into a police car. He believed his dad had hooked up with an ex-girlfriend shortly after getting out of jail and never spoke to Jake again.

A few months later, his mom had a boyfriend who took a liking to Jake. It was refreshing. There were trips to the fair and ballgames. It was all great until he started, as Jake said, "doing things."

Jake abruptly stopped the story there. I could only guess about the "things."

"Did you tell your mom?" I asked.

"She knew. She couldn't do anything," he said, defensively.

"I know, but…"

"No, you don't know, so shut the fuck up."

I did shut the fuck up. And, after that day our friendship faded. He quit his paper route a few weeks later and kept his distance at school. Being a blockheaded teen, I didn't really connect it all back then. I just figured he thought he was better than me, and aimed for a higher social standing. But, it seemed possible now that he'd said too much and regretted it. Hard to know.

He probably felt like I'd look at him differently, and sadly he was right. I saw him as a victim. Broken underneath his false bravado. I watched him become ASB President, but I still saw a beaten and presumably molested child. I felt sorry for him, and he probably hated me for that. Thirty years later, I still thought of him differently than anyone else. I empathized with him, but also felt jealousy as he eased his way out of our friendship.

Even now, I still felt a little of both. For a while, I thought he lived the dream life. Now I could see his was broken. Totaled.

15

GETTING THE POINT

Mallory Facebook post: Glad I watched my step while at Elijah Mound, the high point in the state of Illinois:
Link: Human remains found at Elijah Mound / Chicago Sun-Times

By Scott Johnson
Staff writer

Imagine Dale Wagner's surprise, when the backhoe pulled skeletal remains along with the dirt he was digging for a small construction project.

"At first I figured it was just an animal," said Wagner, a third generation farmer. "Then, we saw a skull and thought maybe we'd hit an old Indian burial ground."

That seems unlikely, according to the Jo Daviess County coroner. Though a full report won't be released for weeks or perhaps months, it is believed that the remains are less than 10 years old.

The news stunned the Wagner family.

"We've lived here all our lives and I just can't imagine how this would happen," Wagner said.

Wagner said he found the remains on a section of his property rarely used, behind a grove of trees in an area covered by tall grass.

Police would not speculate about when or why the remains were deposited on the Wagner Farm. The sparsely populated area is virtually crime free, and no missing persons reports have been filed in the area for the past 10 years according to the Daviess County Sheriff's Office.

The Wagner farmland includes Elijah Mound, which holds the distinction of being the highest natural point of elevation in Illinois. Because of this, Elijah Mound draws dozens of tourists each summer.

"Maybe one of them done it," Wagner said. "The one thing I know is that our family is all alive, and none of them buried anyone back there."

Wagner said he will put his construction project on hold, and will likely choose another location when it resumes.

"I'll tell you one thing," Wagner said. "I'm going to be a little nervous the next time I dig around here."

With bile rising, I read the story knowing full well how those remains found their way to that location. I'd been waiting for Jake's next mention of a high point. Weeks had passed since our meeting at the lake house. Nothing. He'd either stopped high-pointing or kept it a secret.

During the spring, while I was in my classroom being a crappy teacher, I'd read a lot about serial killers, state high points and the people who become high pointers.

Jake's background fit the profile. Many serial killers blamed their mothers, often fairly, for their childhood misery. At some point they realized that one person they thought should give a shit, really didn't. Or couldn't. Jake, by my estimation, seemed smarter than your average serial killer. They often baffled police for years, earning a legendary, genius status as they eluded capture. When caught, they underwhelmed with limited intelligence and social skills. People expected a raving lunatic, not the guy next door. Jake seemed different in that regard. Then again, he was the only one I'd ever met.

He did seem to fit in as a high pointer. It takes a person with varied interests to climb to the highest point in each state. It's not just for hikers and climbers. Many high points are no more than a few steps away from a parking lot. I've faced more obstacles getting from parking lot to cash register at the grocery store than I would at some high points.

Out west, things start to get much more complicated. Though some are said not to be difficult trails, the elevation alone can be a problem for many. A mile can feel like 10, and altitude sickness can cripple anyone–even avid runners in top physical condition. You don't really know how it will impact you until you get there, and just because you didn't get it one time doesn't mean you won't the next.

High Pointers weren't usually parents of young children, though they didn't fit one category, either. Online I found a list of people who'd completed all 50. And, yes, I stalked some of their Facebook pages. It seemed like a good chunk of them, though, fell into three categories:

1. Subaru Forester-driving DINKs: These were dual-income-no-kids people who made decent money and had nowhere to spend it. They weren't rich, so the trips to Europe were limited. And, they weren't

tropical vacationers–that's just sooooo cliché... (I wish I could afford that cliché.) They also love checking things off lists and are mountain climbers or wannabe climbers. From reading a few hiking blogs, it seemed some DINKs make it to 45 summits and stop there. They get cold on Mt. Hood in Oregon. They get the piss scared out of them on the way to Borah's Peak in Idaho and realize they'll never be able to handle Denali. I thought about how much it would suck to spend all that time, money and effort to fall five short. That must be why I stopped at one. Right...

2. Second-lifers: In their early 50s and in peak condition. They've done marathons, maybe even triathlons. They've taken enough "normal" vacations to be bored with them. Now, it's time to see the United States, the healthy way! This will never happen to me. I promise.
3. Serial killers: OK, this is a new category. And only one person in it so far. But this category proved to be my only concern.

It seemed like many of them topped one high point and became hooked. Wouldn't it be fun to do them all? I didn't understand it at all, though I sort of felt that way about brewpubs. That's a hobby I could love.

I took another look at Jake's state high points album on his Facebook page. According to his color-coded map, like most people, he was saving the six most difficult and expensive for last: Oregon (Mt. Hood, 11,239 feet), Idaho (Borah Peak, 12,662), Montana (Granite Peak, 12,799), Gannett Peak (Wyoming, 13,804), Washington (Mt. Rainier, 14,411) and Alaska (Denali, also known as Mt. McKinley, 20,320)

He'd gone in a way that seemed out-of-order, hitting California, Utah and Arizona a few years back–way before many of the easier East Coast jaunts. I didn't check, but I surmised this trip coincided with a UW football away game or two.

Outside of the Big 6, only Colorado (Mt. Elbert, 14,440) and New Mexico (Wheeler Peak, 13,161) remained.

I thought about his list of completed high points and wondered how many he had killed. There was no way it was a 1-to-1 ratio. There were many cases where he'd been to several high points in one day. Was it one per trip? Just when it struck his fancy? What makes a serial killer decide to kill that particular day? Why not every day. Why not never? Was it like a woman deciding to have sex with her husband? A seemingly arbitrary pattern to the husband, but logical to the wife?

I shivered.

How did he do it, exactly? I wondered. There was no way he was hauling a dead human body all the way up to the summit.

Did he make them hike at gunpoint? Chop them.... I couldn't finish the thought.

I thought through the gunpoint thing. Even for a guy who clearly thought he could charm, outsmart and manipulate anyone, this was too big of a risk. Someone would read the body language of a woman being led to her imminent death. Too many potential eye witnesses.

Chopping... I didn't see that one happening, either. I didn't see any giant backpacks in his photos. And, even the skinniest jogger mom still weighs over 100 pounds. More for witnesses to see. Potential leaking...

Did he kill them and bury them along the early part of the trail? That one made the most sense to me. You kidnap a woman, kill her and put her in the trunk of a rental car. Go to a remote destination, and find an even more remote destination. Most of the high points are in the middle of nowhere. Even the more popular ones are near vast areas of unadulterated nature.

Elijah Mound was unique. The hike was nothing, but the highest natural point in Illinois (a Sears Tower elevator ride would take you higher than Elijah Mound's 1,235 feet of elevation) was located on private property. From what I'd read, the Wagners were nice folks, but they didn't want people traipsing across their farmland every day. So, they opened it up for a few weekends each summer.

Jake reached the top of Elijah Mound on June 2, 2016. Two years later, human remains "less than 10 years old" were found on Elijah Mound.

Only Jake and I knew why they were there.

I went to the *Chicago Sun-Times* website, and searched "missing mother." Below a few faces of missing children, an article from June 2016 made it clear to me who'd just been dug up: Allison Rogers.

Rockford Woman "Simply Vanished"
By Chris Beatty
Staff writer

Rockford–According to a source within the Rockford Police Department, police have no leads in the disappearance of missing mother Allison Rogers.

"She simply vanished," said the source, who requested anonymity due to the ongoing investigation.

Rogers did not arrive to pick up her three children at Spring Valley Elementary at the end of the school day on Thursday, immediately setting off alarm bells for friends and family members.

"She's a fantastic mother," said Deanna Goss. "She would never forget to pick up her kids. She was never even a minute late, especially when it involved her children."

A reward fund of $50,000 for any information leading to Rogers' whereabouts has been established. Police can be reached via 9-1-1, or the Allison Rogers hotline, (815) 555-1511.

A second article, which featured a professional head shot of Rogers, went on to talk about how great she was–perfect mom, wife and community member. She's helped raise money for a new playground at her kids' school. Helped in the classroom, and everyone loved her. Another mother-of-the-year no one wanted dead. Except Jake.

I ran across another article, this one written nearly a year before she disappeared. The story, from a small weekly paper, described her tenacity in getting that new, safe playground built at the school. I wondered if that article opened the door to her death. Perhaps Jake found that story and saw the mother he'd never have.

What would the article say if I went missing? There'd probably be no article. I wasn't pretty or accomplished enough for that. I could see the headline:

Guy Who Never Did Anything Disappeared a Long Time Ago and No One Noticed.

Rogers' remains, assuming they were the ones found at Elijah Mound, had not been identified. The article Jake linked in his Facebook post did not even mention whether they were male or female or for sure how long they had been there.

I again found myself trying to rationalize. Maybe Elijah Mound is located on an old Indian burial ground? A Civil War cemetery? No, the article said probably less than 10 years, and they wouldn't be off by that much.

"No," I said to my naked ice cubes. "Jake, we both know it's Allison Rogers."

Again, I started thinking about who would be next. This had to stop. I didn't know how, but I couldn't live with myself if he killed another one. This had to stop.

16

WAITING

Rhonda Facebook post: Im so ready for the school year to start. Get these kid's out of here so I can put this house back together!

It had been a long summer. As a teacher, this is normally a wonderful thing. But not this time. Jake was quiet on Facebook for much of the summer. No high points, or at least none that he mentioned. Though pleased he might not be killing anyone, the wait was agonizing. I knew it wasn't over. I was just waiting around for someone to die.

It was maddening. The waiting. The helplessness. The gutlessness. All of it.

I'd tried to tell two people I knew well. One thought I was kidding, the other thought I was nuts. If I took this story to a police station, they'd kindly point me toward a psych eval. I considered stalking Jake, leaving my wife and kids behind for a week to follow his every move. But, even if I found a way to do this for a week, would anything come from it?

I hoped that he would just stop. And, as the summer sun drifted away, I began to wonder. With no posts about high points all summer, I almost started to think that was possible. Was there a chance that our conversation at the lake scared him straight?

The new school year began, and I immersed myself in work and kids sports, and the occasional growler from the beer store. Life began drifting back toward a normal October. Then, suddenly, it wasn't.

17

VERY BAD IDEA

Mallory facebook post: Time to get the Lead(ville) out!

79 people reacted this

Evelyn Watson: Where are you off to now?

Ron Diaz: Dude, do you ever go to work?

Josh Simmons: Leadville… sounds exotic.

Kristin Hughes: Must be high-pointing again.

Jake Mallory: You win, Kristin Hughes! Mt. Elbert: 14,440 feet. It was 14,433 feet before the USGS reevaluated the elevation. Glad I waited for my extra 7 feet!

Evelyn Watson: I haven't seen you post about climbing for a while. Getting lazy?

Jim Lamb: Going to UW-CO?

Jake Mallory: No, Evelyn Watson, I had to take a couple of months off. Minor knee scope. Just started running again a few weeks ago and am ready to take another stab at it. Yes, Jim, Lamb, I think the knee injury was the football gods' way of telling me to wait until October for Elbert so I could make a little side trip to Boulder!

A knee injury. That explained the hiatus. I'd hoped that maybe he'd found a good shrink and talked out his need to kill–if he was killing. I still hoped I was the one who was nuts instead of him. It's usually easier to be nuts than figure shit out and have to deal with it.

But, he was back, and, "ready to take another stab at it." Another stab. Just a figure of speech, right? What a weekend this would be! Catch the game and kill someone's mother, LOL!

Jake didn't know it, but I was coming along for the trip. All I had to do was run it by my wife, a task that seemed just as daunting as chasing a killer.

"You're going to think I'm crazy...," I nervously said to Kathleen on a Monday.

"Way ahead of you there," she said without looking up from her laptop.

"I need to talk to you about this. I know you'll think I'm crazy, but I'm going to Colorado this weekend."

She looked up from her screen, took a deep breath and sucked her lips into her teeth. I knew this look–the "here's why you're being an idiot" look. I hated that look, but knew her batting average was pretty good when she offered it. I probably was being an idiot.

"Uh, why?"

I'd planned to tell her the truth–lay it all out there. I really did–I'd even rehearsed it.

"You know my buddy, Adam?" I audibled.

"Yeah."

"He's got some free tickets to the UW-Colorado game, and he invited me to go."

She studied me closely. Like a therapist I should probably be seeing instead of taking this trip.

"We can't afford it," she said while lightly shaking her head.

"I know–but it's going to be super-cheap. Did you hear me say, 'free?' Another buddy of his was going to go, but can't. So, he's on the hook for most of it. I'll take on some extra duties at school to cover it."

"Yeah, you have about as much time as money," she said, head moving back toward the computer. "This is a bad idea."

No shit, I thought. *You have no fucking idea how bad.*

"Hey, you can finally have a little alone time," I offered, gingerly.

Her head stayed facing the screen, but her eyes moved toward me for a quick glare. This look usually didn't mean good things for me.

"Yeah, OK, I guess," she said, accepting a surprisingly easy defeat.

With me out of the picture she would be alone for a few days. The kids had a long weekend–it was Columbus Day but the schools weren't calling it that any more–and were leaving on Thursday to camp with their grandparents. I figured Kathleen would busy herself with a couple of her divorced friends. I hoped she wouldn't be joining them permanently.

To cover my ass, I called Adam, a college friend who lived a few hours away. Thankfully, no Facebook for him. I chose him because Kathleen didn't like him much and a conversation between the two was unlikely. Divorced twice and justifiably so, he wasn't the best influence. Just in case she contacted Adam, I explained to him that I was having an affair and needed him to cover for me if Kathleen called for some reason. It was kind of a dumb idea, but at the moment it seemed smarter than telling him I was stalking a serial killer.

Adam briefly tried to talk me out of cheating on my wife–explaining that my wife was already too hot for me. It was a weak effort on his part, considering he'd gone down the road many times himself.

"Dude, this is a bad idea," he said.

No shit, I thought again.

"I know, dude. Probably the dumbest idea I've ever had. You have no idea how dumb. But, I've gotta do it."

The dude logic sunk in, and he sighed.

"She's at least hot, right?"

"So hot."

"Alright, bro, I've got you covered. Don't screw this up."

I booked the trip on a credit card I'd never used, hoping Kathleen wouldn't see it on a statement. I'd just as soon stab myself in the leg as push the "confirm" button, but it could have been worse. I thanked Jake for traveling outside of peak tourism season. A $379 chunk for the flight. Another $200 for a crappy hotel in Leadville. Plus $179 for a Chevy Spark, which looked to be the size of my carry-on.

"There must be a better way to figure out what he's doing," I said to no one. I imagined a curious fool from ancient times looking into the mouth of a volcano to see what was making all the noise. A guy running into a sliding glass door to test its strength, and another looking down a gun barrel to see if it was loaded. These people were like geniuses compared to me at this moment.

I boarded an October-rain-soaked plane headed for Denver on a Wednesday. Jake was flying on Thursday, and I thought it best that we not have a reunion above the clouds.

I hate flying. I'm not the smallest guy in the world, and also I'm not into small talk. Despite my vague understanding of the physics that allow flight to happen, it was not easy to convince myself that a 150,000-pound metal object containing hundreds of likely victims and all their most important crap could just cruise along at 35,000 feet without landing nose-first into the side of a mountain.

I really needed a drink. But, of all the cruel tragedies in the world, the worst was that I would puke if I even sniffed a beer in an airplane. Altitude or nerves, I wasn't sure. But, the barf bag needed to stay tucked away in its upright position for this trip.

I found seat 18B–my reward for the late flight reservation was a seat between a guy in a business suit and another in a sweat suit. I sat between them in something lovely from my shorts and baseball jacket collection and jockeyed for armrest position. I silently vowed to not move my right elbow for the next three hours.

The three of us, linked only by our proximity for the next three hours, did a marvelous job of ignoring each other's existence. I appreciated them very much. While generally friendly, I preferred silence. Maybe it's because the opportunity for silence is so rare, or maybe it's an only child thing.

And, again, I have that face. The one that for reasons well beyond my control appears to be wide open for babble. One look at me and people assume I'm the guy who'd just love to talk to you about nothing on a plane. Except I'm not.

I went to great lengths to avoid conversation. Headphones connected to nothing. I'd learned that a book would not suffice, but it took a serious windbag to flag you down from your headphone ride. I would pretend to sleep even if I couldn't sleep. I'd not hear greetings I actually heard to keep that conversation door closed.

So, the men sitting to my immediate left and right were silent heroes. I loved them like brothers. I bought the in-flight Wi-Fi, and started researching Leadville and Mt. Elbert.

At first glance, it seemed Leadville should change its name to Deadville, and Mt. Elbert was pretty easy to hike unless you liked oxygen. One of those first impressions was correct.

The beverage cart came by, and I ordered a ginger ale. I'd ordered the same thing every time since my first flight at age 9, and no plane with me as a passenger had ever crashed. I had no interest in determining if it was, in fact, the ginger ale that kept me airborne.

I dozed off, falling deeply enough to dream. I was walking on the edge of a cliff. Rocks tumbled down the side as my feet pushed them over the edge. Each time I stumbled and barely caught myself just before the earth gave way and sucked me into its belly. I kept moving forward. In the dream I never considered going back. That's why dreams are dumb. With each step, the ledge became more brittle. I toed the brittle rock in front of me, and watched it fall straight down into the fog. I heard the rock hit the side of a canyon, skipping into the abyss. With the step in front of me disintegrated, I had no choice but to make a short leap to a firmer-looking ledge a few feet ahead. I jumped, and felt the rock crumble beneath my foot.

"I'm not in your space, bitch!"

Awakened from my fall, I gasped for air, earning acknowledgment of my existence by way of awkward glances from my row buddies.

I choked down a couple of gulps of air, feeling relief for the first time ever that I was in an airplane. So far, it wasn't falling from the sky. As my pulse slowed, I regained my faculties and could see that the passengers who had awakened me weren't sharing the armrest very nicely. They were on the other side of the aisle, one row ahead.

"See this? This right here?," said a woman of about 50. "This is my space. That is your space!"

She had a strong build and long white hair, which was generally only found on strong-willed women incapable of being wrong about anything.

"I'm. Not. In. Your. Space," he said, with jagged pauses between each word.

He was about 6 inches taller and wider than me. Maybe 10 years younger, but not young enough to wear his ball cap backwards.

"Aren't you going to say anything?" she asked the poor bastard on the other side of her, presumably her husband. She said it like she was asking a 4-year-old to stop eating his own boogers. Smaller than his wife, he looked at her with eyes that said, "I like your chances better than mine."

A hard-faced flight attendant who looked like she'd slap her man in the face while riding him, took control. She looked at the guy confidently, like she knew something he didn't. Like she could push a button and send him shooting out of the ass of the plane. Two against one, the fat guy lost his aisle seat and scurried toward the front of the plane.

"I didn't do anything," he whined, like a third-grader who'd touched the hair of the girl in front of him too many times. In his mind, the first-class seat he'd earned was not proper restitution for his loss in the Battle of the Armrest.

18

Risky Business

Colorado

The reward outweighed the risk, he reminded himself as he finalized his plans. She lived too close to the mountain, but he wanted her even more than the others. He needed this one. It had been far too long and she fit the profile beautifully.

Long ago she escaped the farm to become a successful business owner. An advocate for children in the backward town, the article said while glossing over the fact that she essentially used her own children as slave labor.

That's what would get her killed. A beautiful two-hour window between when she arrived home and left her kids to close down the restaurant. Though he'd be putting himself too close to the crime this time, he'd never be spotted. She lived, for now, far out of sight and and this would be easy.

As he packed his gear, he thought for a moment about his dumbass classmate who'd asked some interesting questions. One more question would force him to change course. Not yet, though. The mountaintop called for him.

19

DEADVILLE

Colorado

churchofcannibals Facebook post: Don't buy a Prius to save the planet's resources. Kill yourself!

Squares of green, brown and tan with jagged peaks looming ominously in the distance greeted the occupants of the airplane as it descended slowly toward a Denver International Airport runway.

Those mountains. What exactly was my plan here? My answer was vague and stupid. I was going to locate and follow him, doing my best fat-man-Chevy-Spark-driving Magnum P.I.

If I failed to find him on Thursday, I would park at the Mt. Elbert trail entrance. I'd stake it out, binoculars, thermos and all.

Aside from no Ferrari and no T.C. to fly me around the mountain, the Magnum P.I. stakeout method faced a major problem: There were five trails used to summit Elbert, according to summitpost.org. Most people used either the North or South Mt. Elbert Trailheads. More experienced hikers often elected to try the South Halfmoon Creek Trailhead, the Black Cloud Trailhead or the Echo Canyon Trailhead.

I closed my eyes. What would Jake do? Other than kill people? Based on the Facebook comment discussions he'd had, it appeared this was his first time to Elbert and he'd be hiking it alone a few months after minor knee surgery. The snow hadn't hit yet, but it would be cold and icy in places.

During one of my sleepless nights, I'd thought about the mechanics of killing a woman and burying her. I Googled a bit, and found some sick fuckers on the Internet more than willing to give a person all the info they needed about decomposition rates, in all types of climates. Churchofcannibals.com offered a step-by-step guide about how to turn humans into choice cuts.

This led to several more sleepless nights. Based on simple logic and also the body found at Elijah Mound, Jake clearly wasn't burying victims right next to the sign at the highest point of the high point. It seemed likely that two hikes with adjacent destinations occurred.

The women I suspected Jake of killing were not large, but not waifs, either. He wasn't going to haul 100-plus pounds 4.6 miles while gaining nearly a mile in elevation. I remembered a Dateline episode in which a detective said, "They call it 'dead weight' for a reason." I'd even talked my 10-year-old son, Mason, into pretending to be dead. I tried to pick up his 100-pound body with limited success. I'd dragged the kid around the living room, causing his hair to stand straight up from carpet-against-head static. It was much more difficult that I'd imagined. After a few minutes, we both tumbled to the floor and giggled.

"See, that's why you don't want to kill me," I said. "Too hard to move."

If my research was correct, Jake's victims usually disappeared in the evening. He probably killed them fairly quickly, and waited until nightfall to dump or bury the body at a secluded location in the vicinity of a high point trail. So, two hikes: One at night when it was crucial to not be seen with a body. A second one when he summited the high point while taking selfies. A microcosm of Jake's seemingly dual personality.

Between social media, map websites and other information found online, Jake could probably plan his entire day without ever leaving home. He could pick out his victims by using social media, newspaper articles, online PTA newsletters, etc. You could even figure out when her kids had baseball practice if you snooped enough. I'd read an article about how thieves used social media to learn when people left their homes unattended. That family photo with frightened faces at Splash Mountain serves as a "vacant" sign on your home. Perhaps this process could be used to figure out when a woman was alone.

Just swoop in, verify locations and pounce on a victim. The getaway car was a nondescript rental, making DNA evidence about as useful as fluids found in a rent-by-the-hour motel room. With each crime taking place in a different state, it seemed unlikely law enforcement would establish a link. Only my dumbass bad luck had uncovered it.

I could hear Albert King singing, "Lord, if it wasn't for bad luck, I wouldn't have no luck at all."

I considered which trail Jake would choose. While he liked to do things his own way–especially to make a point that he can do things his own way–I believed he'd play it a bit safely and go with the North trail. A quick drive from Leadville, it seemed to offer the fastest route, great views and was well-traveled enough to offer safety in numbers.

The body wouldn't go to that trail, however. Or at least not on the same day. Or maybe no public trail at all. The vastness of undeveloped land around Mt. Elbert overwhelmed me.

I had to find Jake on Thursday. Thursday: Kill. Friday: Hike to relive and celebrate. Saturday: Football game. It was Thursday or nothing. If I could witness him kidnapping a woman and call the police, then I could give them all my research. They could at least nail him for kidnapping and would hopefully look for proof of larger crimes. My biggest concerns were that a woman could be killed before the police responded, or that he'd figure out he was being followed. The latter could lead to bad things for me. I would have to stay way off him and hope that he was too overconfident to look in his rearview mirror.

I considered staking out the airport, but there were many flights spread out amongst many airlines. Only one road to Leadville, however. I'd find a spot on the side of the road. Watch every car go by until I found him.

My brilliant planning was interrupted by the yelp from the airplane tires hitting the runway. It seemed like the captain was hitting the brakes awfully hard, and I briefly imagined us crashing into the side of the airport. We coasted to the gate, though, and the captain eventually shut it down and turned off the seatbelt sign. I stood up way too early–why did I always do this? Unwilling to admit my mistake and reclaim my seat, I stood hunched over and watched 17 rows in front of me take their sweet-ass time pulling their carry-ons from above and stumbling down the plank-sized aisle.

"He better not say anything to me," the Battle of the Armrest winner said. Her husband nodded, sighed and pretended to give a shit.

Good luck, buddy, I muttered to myself.

I left my rear-of-the-plane captors behind and entered the terminal, stepping on a moving walkway and side-stepping past a family enjoying the ride. I watched a plane taxi directly toward the building, and felt a sense of relief when I realized it wasn't going to crash into it. I turned around in time to see it exit through the tunnel on the other side of the terminal, wondering if that part of the building plan was really necessary.

The final moving walkway dumped me into food-court hell. I tried to talk myself out of a chocolate cream-filled from Dunkin Donuts, a chain that had left the Seattle market a couple of years after Jake and I last hung out there. Failed. I hitched a shuttle ride to go pick up my Spark.

I squeezed in the car and managed to avoid two speed traps along Pena Boulevard, then headed west on I-70. It was early afternoon, and the traffic was light.

Downtown Denver greeted me with an odor that smelled like someone had eaten dog food, guzzled cheap beer and then vomited it all on old running shoes. As I passed Denver Coliseum, I could see Mile High Stadium and Coors Field in the distance. It was October, so no danger of baseball happening there. I wished they were playing, so there could be an excuse to call off this entirely fruitless plan and go to a baseball game instead.

Despite the stench and typical urban industrial decay, the city looked beautiful. Skyscrapers waved goodbye as I left downtown, though they appeared diminutive compared to the mountains that surrounded me.

Denver differed from many large cities I'd seen. It looked like it had been scooped up out of a megalopolis and dropped in the middle of nowhere. It seemed out of place. I could relate.

As the population density lessened exponentially with each mile, I headed toward the highest point the Rockies had to offer.

I passed an old reader board–one that had lost some letters over the years.

CUM $EE ARE H GE S L CTI0N!

I chuckled, remembering my lone attempt at changing a reader board. Eighth grade, Jake and I snuck out in the middle of the night. We rode our bikes up to Highway 99, not far from where the Green River Killer stalked his prey. We found a reader board, and decided to rewrite it. When the police officer yelled "freeze!" I dropped the letters F, C and K at my feet.

My mom picked me up at the police station, and needless to say that was not a good few weeks for me. She already disliked Jake, and our trip together to the station meant I wasn't supposed to go anywhere near him ever again. Of course that just meant I lied about where I hung out for the next few months, until Jake cut that cord on his own. She already didn't like me running around town, fearing that the Green River Killer would catch me, even though I wasn't a female prostitute.

Ah, the Green River killer. The man who terrorized the area around SeaTac Airport in the early 1980s. It seemed like every time I watched the news as a kid, they talked about another body of a young woman being found just a few miles from my home. I remember riding my bike along the Green River Trail, eyes wandering into the water to see if there was anyone in there.

One of the saddest things about tragedy is the ripple of fear it creates. Women of all ages, prostitutes or not, were afraid to leave their homes during that time. Our entire region was obsessed with the Green River Killer. None more that Jake.

"It's got to be the janitor," he said to me one day. "You know, the one who always has the cigar hanging out of his mouth. Have you seen the way he stares at people?"

We all had our theories and it was often at the forefront of our minds. But, Jake was an expert on the subject. He knew many of the victims' names, and was fascinated by their suspected profession–prostitution.

On another night when we sneaked out of our homes, we walked toward a section of Highway 99 called Pacific Highway South, now called International Boulevard. We walked silently along the roads, diving behind bushes when we saw headlights. We were on a mission: To see a real-life prostitute. As we approached 99, Jake's eyes widened with excitement.

"He could have grabbed one from right there," he said, pointing toward the darkened, four-lane highway. "He can just grab one whenever he wants. They just get right in his car and then he kills them!"

We got a little closer to the highway. I expected to see a line of women walking down the side of the road, like zombies. I saw nothing but the passing of an occasional car that forced our retreat.

"He's got to be some sort of fucked-up genius," he said. "He's killed all those women, and they can't catch him. All those police looking for him, and nothing. A fucking genius, dude."

It's funny how much different it sounded playing back through my head that day in Colorado. Now, it seemed like much more than boyhood curiosity–the same curiosity I'd held. Hell, every memory I had of Jake now seemed like a precursor to killing that I had missed. As for Jake's hero, cops finally busted the Green River Killer in 2001. Another murderer brought down by the advent of cold-case DNA analysis, it turned out that he wasn't all that bright. The killer, Gary Ridgeway, was a truck painter with a below-average IQ who had mostly evaded arrest by dumb luck. He was sentenced to life in prison when he calmly testified to killing 48 women. He's admitted to killing at least 71 overall. I wondered what Jake thought of Ridgeway's downfall. Such an inglorious end to an infamous villain.

I shook away the memory and tried to refocus as all hints of civilization became more and more scant along the highway. I began to see why they called them the Rocky Mountains. Everything around me appeared Rocky. Like it could crumble at any moment and I'd land in a pile of broke Precambrian metamorphic rock.

Signs of civilization again. I passed a high school field–*Home of the Gold Diggers!*–and drove through the Idaho Springs tunnel. Another sign said, *Idaho Springs–Where It All Began!!* A reference to the Pike's Peak Gold Rush of 1859.

The Eisenhower-Johnson Memorial tunnel brought me back to the west side of the Continental Divide. The combination of a nearly 2-mile tunnel and the 11,000-plus feet of elevation took my breath away.

Just south of Frisco (not that Frisco), I exited I-70 and headed south on Highway 91. Each turn brought a new view, an eminence art gallery tour.

A couple of ski towns and a mountain pass later, I floated into Leadville alongside the headwaters of the Arkansas River.

A smattering of houses and barns began rising up from the rocks as I neared the old mining town. The drive had been enlightening. Colorado seemed caught between moving toward the future and reliving its mining past. I thought of the Brady Bunch getting jailed in an old ghost town. Would Jake lock me in an old prison and make off with my Spark? He'd probably rather walk than be seen in that glorified tricycle.

The area around Leadville drew prospectors during the Pike's Peak gold rush, but the town boomed in the mid-1870s when silver-lead deposits were discovered nearby. They called it Slabville for a while, and then changed it to Leadville when the city began to boom. By 1880, it was the second-largest city in Colorado with approximately 14,000 citizens. Doc Holliday lived there for a while, and Oscar Wilde was among its visitors.

Like many old Colorado towns, the mines dried up, and the surrounding beauty wasn't enough to feed most of its metal-hungry citizens. The city was home to 2,602 residents according to the 2010 census.

It wasn't a ghost town, but it had declined enough to earn the nickname "Deadville." I expected nothing, which left room for pleasant surprise. I had assumed Leadville was another mining town whose time came and went over a century ago. While it was that in many ways, Leadville turned out to be a place I might like to visit sometime when I wasn't trying to stop women from being murdered.

My mind drifted as I approached downtown Leadville. I pictured a *Seattle Times* story describing the death of someone's mother. And me, I was dead too, in this story. One word stuck out in the headline of this fictional–or perhaps foreboding–news story.

Deadville.

I glanced to my left, gloomy thoughts abrogated by a 50-foot wide sign that read, "WE (heart) LEADVILLE. GREAT LIVING @10,200'"

I giggled. Yes, giggled. I felt a little drunk, the altitude getting to my head. I could see Mt. Elbert and neighboring Mt. Massive as I turned left on Harrison Avenue into the heart of downtown. I remembered reading about the two mountains. Years ago, there had been much debate about which mountain stood taller. Mt. Massive was, well, more massive because of its summit ridge of over three miles. In the late 1800s when the mountains were surveyed, it was determined that Mt. Elbert beat out Massive by 12 feet. In the Great Depression era, Mt. Massive supporters actually piled rocks in an effort to overtake Elbert only to have them knocked over by rival Elbertians.

I wasn't sure what I expected of Leadville. Tumbleweeds? Crumbled buildings? Long-bearded ghosts walking the streets? Instead, a refurbished downtown welcomed me. A mix of the past and the present. A town that embraced its beginnings while serving as home to those who worked in nearby ski towns.

I pulled into the pothole-laden driveway to my crappy hotel. The summer tourists were gone, and the fall hikers were dwindling. The skiers were a few weeks away yet, so I nearly had the place to myself.

"Hello, sir, do you have a reservation?" the desk clerk asked.

"Yes, four nights."

She was polite but moved quickly as if a line suddenly sprouted behind me.

"Oh, hello, Mr. Peddin. Only one I've got coming in today."

In the room I could see that the place probably wasn't going to kill me, and the room offered a view of Mt. Elbert out my dingy window. Not bad for $49 a night.

A little later, I drove through town again and picked my stakeout spot, the parking lot of a discount store. A decent number of people there, but I didn't think it was Jake's kind of place. I assumed he'd drive past it sometime the next day, and I would tail him from there.

I spent the evening in my room eating take-out and watching the Major League Baseball playoffs.

I watched a 5-foot-6-inch player crush a series-winning homer. He was able to filter out the pressure, and even the annoying sound of someone banging on a garbage can. I knew he was a great player, but I again marveled at the guy. No one ever thought he'd make it to the Big Leagues, and here he was taking down the mighty New York Yankees.

So far in life I had part down about no one ever expecting me to amount to anything. Was there any chance I could ever channel some of this player's ability to win at all costs? It seemed unlikely. If I could just get on base somehow and let the cops drive me in to take down the mighty Jake Mallory. That's all I needed. "Don't try to do too much," I said out loud. "Just go with the pitch." Knowing what pitch is coming, though, sure would be helpful.

I'd felt the altitude riding in the car. It took hold even ascending one flight of stairs in the motel. It ate me up during the night. I faded in and out of consciousness, gasping for air each time I awoke. Great living at 10,200 feet, my ass. I clearly was not built for this.

I drained the continental breakfast room of all its coffee and pocketed a banana that was in the process of skipping yellow to go straight from green to brown. I lumbered to my Spark and drove to my stakeout point. Caffeine and anticipation flowed through my veins and I felt more awake than ever despite a spotty night of sleep.

I pulled into a space facing the highway and placed a baseball cap on my head. Then wondered if that looked suspicious. I evaluated the Chevy Spark. Thankfully silver, but so small it stood out.

Then, I waited.

And waited.

Stakeouts were fucking boring.

I needed a smart-ass sidekick, someone who pissed me off but passed the time. He could make fat jokes and remind me that I was an old man. I'd explain to him that he was making the same dumbass mistakes as me, and he'd better toe the line if he expected to go anywhere in the police department.

Or, like a good TV detective, maybe I could see something I wasn't supposed to see that would take this case in a whole new direction. Like, maybe Gary Ridgeway had escaped and was following Jake around while killing women. Or Jake was The Eraser, a guy who helped women disappear from their boredom, leaving no trace behind. I liked that one because no one died.

Instead, nothing. Hours passed. Cars passed. The temperature climbed from freezing to pleasant. I listened to classic rock on the radio. I stared at the road, sizing up every car that passed.

Finally, there he was. I could see him in a small SUV wearing a white hat, his hiking backpack standing up in the back seat. So, he did have a big backpack… . I pulled out slowly, leaving plenty of distance and a semi between us. We cruised down Harrison, following Highway 24 as it turned right on 9th and left on Poplar heading out of the other side of town.

He pulled into the Safeway parking lot. I thought this was odd–not sure that would be my first stop. He exited the car, with his back facing me and opened the rear door. He appeared to be fiddling with his backpack for unreasonably long, and then… . Shit.

He pulled a baby out of the car seat. Not a backpack, but a car seat. I cursed myself. Up close this guy looked nothing like Jake. The fucking white hat and boredom had blinded me.

I stared at him like he was a criminal. Sensing my vitriol, he looked up at me and then quickly away. Then a sideways glance as he wondered why a nut stared him down in the Safeway parking lot.

I drove back through town to the discount store. My head turned with each car, like the dog falling for a boy's lame pump fake over and over.

I gave up as the sun sank behind Mt. Elbert. During those few minutes I'd chased the red herring, I had missed him.

If it wasn't for bad luck, I wouldn't have no luck at all.

Back in town, I cruised the motel parking lots looking for signs of Jake.

Nothing.

I parked, lowered my cap down to my eyebrows and began a fruitless search through town, amazed how much the altitude hindered my progress. I ducked my head in several restaurants. I stopped at the Silver Dollar Saloon and downed a shot of Jameson, a beautiful burn.

By now all of the souvenir shops had closed. Though the mountains had been emptied a hundred years ago, it seemed like every other building sold jewelry made in Leadville.

Deadville.

Along with my awareness that I had just wasted my time, money and marriage for nothing, I realized that I was starving. Nothing but coffee and a few bites of a banana all day. Anyone who ever looked at me would know that's unusual. I hoped to find something open off the main drag.

I walked past the Tabor Opera House, built in 1879, now sitting next to a Kum & Go mini-mart. What would

Mr. Tabor think of that now? Posters for shows the past summer hung in the window. Paula Poundstone. She was still doing her thing, eh? Sorry I missed it.

I crossed the street and glanced down 4th Street, eyes focusing on a pizza place.

Perfect. Jake wasn't going to Leadville for pizza. He'd choose Miner Mike's Bar and Grill for some prime rib, or something like that. He'd want something a miner would have eaten after striking it rich. The pizza place was far enough off the main drag, and I figured no one ever died from pizza.

Rocky Mountain Pie sat on the verge of a neighborhood. A glorified double-wide marked only by a nearly illegible sign and a neon slice of pizza tattooed to the front of the building. Use of too many bright colors made it stand out on the street and perhaps from the top of Mt. Elbert.

A cute, but bored teenage girl looked up as I opened the door. A streak of blue ran through her blonde hair. She looked like someone planning to get out of Leadville the moment her clock struck 18.

Slam!

I jumped.

The door, missing is spring mechanism, shut hard behind me. She smiled, a mixture of *ha-ha, gotcha and it happens all the time.* I wondered how many people went airborne when they walked in to Rocky Mountain Pie for the first time, like an alarm trap set for folks not from around those parts.

On auto-pilot again, she said hello and handed me a menu.

A little rattled and unsure what to order, I could feel a stare coming from the corner table. I didn't look–I was in no mood for small talk. Again, that stupid face of mine.

The one that promised something that didn't exist in my insides. I looked at names of pizzas that made no sense, The Crocodile, The Aussie, The Pirate....

I could still feel the stare. I tried to decide whether to ignore it or look back at the person deliberately, hopefully forcing them to turn away.

"Of all the pizza joints in all the world, you walked into mine," said the man staring at me.

Fuck. I thought about ducking my head and walking out to grab something from the Kum & Go. The last thing in the world I wanted was to talk to some cheesy dumbass for 15 minutes while waiting for a pizza.

OK, maybe that was the second to last thing in the world I wanted. The last thing I wanted was worse than I could have imagined.

20

TWO GUYS, A GIRL AND A PIZZA PLACE

Leadville, Colorado

Mallory facebook post: Of all the pizza joints in all of the towns, in all of the world, he walks into mine!–At Rocky Mountain Pie with Bob Peddin.

All day, I'd been obsessively searching for this guy, and he ends up right in front of me. He stared at me like a poker player revealing pocket aces.

He wore a gray baseball cap with no logo, a forest green sweatshirt and jeans. He seemed dressed down. I expected him to either be in full hiking gear, covered in purple Huskies stuff or wearing a Great Living at 10,200 feet T-shirt. He looked, well, kind of like me.

"Holy shit, dude, what are you doing in Leadville?"

It sounded like mock amazement. My heart raced. My mind tried to follow but lost ground quickly.

What ARE you doing here, Bob? I thought.

Hiking? No way. He knew I struggled just climbing stairs to my seats at Husky Stadium. He wouldn't buy hiking.

Visiting a friend or family? Yeah, and going to a pizza place alone.

Just passing through? No one just passed through Leadville. You either had a reason to be there or you didn't.

"Uh, just touring the area," is what came out of my mouth. "You know, uh, for my history class. Wanted to see some of the old mining areas."

I sounded nervous, a liar. Like I was making it up one word at a time, because I was doing exactly that.

Jake stared in my eyes, waiting a beat before offering me a seat and a slice. He moved a shoulder bag off the seat and I sat down, wanting desperately to run.

"Tell ya what, bud, this place alone is worth the trip. Good as gold." Nice gold-rush reference, I thought.

A polite host, he ordered another pizza, this time from an attractive woman in her 40s–presumably the teen's mother. I couldn't help but linger a little bit as I looked up. She looked out of place in a hole-in-the-wall pizza joint. Hair in a ponytail, but glistening. A royal blue pizza apron hung just low enough to display some solid cleavage peeking out of a white T-shirt. It wasn't an obvious display. It was a hint, made to look unintentional, like things had just slipped down a bit. Oops. Just enough to let you know that there was more to her than pizza. I glanced away quickly to avoid being busted.

Jake and I ate and chatted. I felt cornered. I stumbled through a little history of the town, glad I'd read about it on the plane. We talked about Husky football–he was shocked I wasn't going to the game. Leaving tomorrow morning, I lied. I grumbled about how the wife wouldn't let me stay for the game. He nodded while thanking the stars for his autonomy.

"So you came all this way. Isn't it a school week? You skipping?"

He looked at me, or rather studied me, seemingly noting everything down to the arch of my eyebrows. I tried not to shake. I'm a terrible actor and an even worse liar. I pulled it together the best I could. I could feel the hair on my arms stabbing me like needles.

"Well," I stumbled, "they, uh, well, there's, it's a long weekend and they let me take an extra day because it's school-related."

"That's cool," he said, his dark eyes lingering.

"I teach a unit about mining and its impact on the settlement of the American West," I continued, doubling down on my obvious bad hand.

I felt like he was searching every pore. I could feel it, like tiny bugs crawling. I needed to get him back on his favorite subject: Jake Mallory. One more second talking about me and I was going to crack.

"What are you doing here? D-Digging for silver?" I sputtered, an unnaturally quick pace.

"Hiking Mt. Elbert," he said. "But you never know, I just might bring a shovel."

I didn't realize it then, but later I wondered if that was a test. If so, I failed. My eyes widened, and the body language that had often led to me sleeping on the couch or evoking the wrath of umpires cost me again.

"Huh?" I muttered, not really wanting to know.

"You know, to see if there's still any silver in them thar hills," he said, punching me on the shoulder, mildly in an "aw shucks" sort of way.

The conversation lulled, opening the door to suspicion.

"Didn't you see it on Facebook?" he asked.

"Sorry, see what?" I asked, gripped by anxiety.

"That I was coming to Leadville. Didn't you see that?"

"Uh no, guess I was too busy to get on there much," was the best I could muster.

I wanted to sprint out of there, if I could run more than five steps at this altitude without keeling over, but I knew I had to suck it up and play along if any chance remained of selling my lies.

My plan to stop Jake was fucked. Now I just wanted to get out of here without him deciding which hill would be best for burying my body. Maybe I hadn't lied to Adam. Maybe I'd end up on top of a woman after all. In a shared grave.

A couple of slices later–it really was great pizza, and I needed something to shove the bile back down my throat–Jake announced that he had to get to his hotel. An emergency at work, he said, required him to compile some data for a report.

"Gotta get it done so I can hit it early tomorrow," he said.

We each dug for our wallets and started digging for the right combination of bills.

"No way, man," Jake said. "Not happening."

He gave me the stop sign, then extended his hand out to my wallet.

"I'll get this one. You can get the next one, if that huge teacher salary will allow it."

I faked a chuckle and we pushed in our chairs, which made a snorting noise against the dark-stained wooden floor. We stepped toward the door, unsure of each other.

"Thanks for coming," the mom said, busy but hospitable. She appeared to be slowly shutting things down for the night.

"Good stuff," Jake said. "I was going to come back at a later time but now my plans got changed."

He said it while smiling at me. I didn't even want to know what he meant by that. She smiled, and handed a bag of garbage to a teenage boy to take to the dumpster.

"We've got the best Leadville has to offer."

"I don't doubt that one bit," Jake said, suggestively. "Not one bit."

It's funny how everything sounds different when death is involved.

Slam!

Damned screen door got me again. I jumped, again, almost Halloween cat-like.

"You OK big guy?" Jake laughed.

"Yeah, that door got me twice. I think the altitude is making me even dumber that I was already."

He smiled.

"Where you parked?" Jake asked, seeing only his rented Ford SUV on the street.

"Around the corner. I walked around a bit."

"Hop in, I'll give you a ride."

"No, I'm fine."

"Come on, you'll pass out walking back up that hill."

A huge, almost maniacal smile took over his face. He grabbed me around the back of my neck and whipped out his phone.

"Leadville selfie! Smile!"

He snapped the photo while I determined it was likely I'd need to change my pants and throw them away. He again offered a ride.

"I need to walk off some of this pizza."

"Come onnnnn," he smiled. "I won't bite."

I froze. I knew it was abnormal to turn down a lift. Especially for a guy like me, in a place where walking a few blocks is not just a simple stroll. But, he was looking at me in a way he never had. Evaluative. If I got in his car would I ever reach mine alive?

He pushed again, and I got in. I wondered if the Highway 99 prostitutes had this feeling when they go in Gary Ridgeway's truck. Between the altitude and fear my heart thumped like a subwoofer.

"OK, where are you parked?" he asked.

I pointed left as we approached the stop sign. I looked down Harrison Avenue, hoping for traffic. I didn't want him to identify my car. My eyes searched desperately for a store I could pop into so he wouldn't see what I was driving.

Nothing. Deadville. No cars for blocks, and nothing open. Maybe this actually was a ghost town.

"Nice ride!" he said, poking fun at my half-car, before his eyes met mine again. "You'll never catch me in that thing."

He looked at me a little too long. I could feel the bugs on my skin again. Had he always been this creepy?

"Yeah," I grumbled. We said our goodbyes and he pulled away. I kneeled down and screamed, "Fuck! Fuck! Fuck" into my arm, using proper sneeze technique for the new millennium. I'd been made. My car had been made. I was the worst fucking P.I. in the world.

I went to my Facebook page and removed my tag from the photo he'd posted. I was completely screwed if Kathleen saw that post. I didn't bother to follow Jake. I was burned, and he'd be watching for me now. I got in my car and drove back to the pizza place. I didn't want to go back, but I feared I wouldn't be able to live with myself if I didn't secretly see the pizza lady home.

I sat in the car, fighting off sleep until I saw the woman walk out, passing a turn-of-the-century Chevy truck that said "Rocky Mountain Pie" on the side. Perhaps what the teens would drive home.

She hopped in a late-model Suburban and drove out of town, heading east. I followed her as far as I could without becoming a suspect. About two miles South on Highway 24, and then east on 44. Almost no other cars on the road at this point, so I let the distance between us increase.

I turned off my lights as we turned south down a lonely road. The moonlight glistened against the dark ribbons on the road, repaired cracks from the extremes of hot sun and sub-zero temperatures. A half-mile between us now, I watched her turn down a dusty road and pull up to a farmhouse. She had some acreage with pastoral and mountain views. Only the porch light shined at the house, and no other cars were visible. I pulled to the side of the road and waited.

A half-hour later, I saw headlight beams approach from behind outshining the moon and stars. I lowered my head. The last thing I needed was to have to explain why I was stalking the Rocky Mountain Pie lady. That probably wouldn't go over too well in town, especially if they figured out what was going on back in Washington state.

I heard the moan of the tires lower its pitch against the rough pavement as the vehicle approached mine. It slowed, and then stopped. I heard it turn around and pick up speed quickly. My head popped up and I could see the taillights of an SUV. A fucking Ford SUV. My concern turned out to be valid. He was planning to kill the pizza lady.

I turned the key in the ignition and cursed my cheap car choice when I heard the engine's wimpy purr. I pulled a quick U-turn and pushed the gas pedal to the floor with limited results. I followed the taillights in front of me as he drove somewhat tentatively as the lead car on a dark and unfamiliar road. I gained on him slightly, skidding around the turn onto Highway 44. The Spark held its own until we screeched onto Highway 24. That's when my frugality began to cost me. The taillights grew smaller. A steep incline beat down my 98-horsepower Spark and it simply couldn't keep up. A few twists in the road and he was gone.

I drove through Leadville, spotting the Rocky Mountain Pie truck hauling the two teens headed toward home. Somehow, Jake had figured out that he had a window of time when their mother would be at home while the teens cleaned and tucked in Rocky Mountain Pie for the night.

I pulled through the parking lots of every motel in town without any luck. He'd vanished like one of his victims.

I drove back toward the pizza lady's house, finding my spot again on the side of the road. What was going through Jake's mind right now? My only hope was that he assumed I was some sort of voyeur, following the pizza lady home. But, deep down I knew he wouldn't see me as a peeper. He had to know I suspected him of murder, and of the planned murder of the owner of Rocky Mountain Pie. I could go home but there was no going back now. And I still had absolutely no proof and no hope.

I saw the glint of the pizza truck's chrome trim in front of the house. I dozed on and off until 3 a.m. There was no sign of any other vehicles, and I decided my pizza lady was safe for the night. I might have saved her, at least for now, but was Jake hauling someone else's mother into the woods? One woman alive for one night with no promises about tomorrow.

21

Now What?

Leadville, Colorado

Kathleen Peddin Facebook post: It's so nice that Bob's taking a guys' weekend. I feel like a widow, though, and I just might be if he decides to do this again! ;)

I spent the next two days in Leadville, searching the town during the day and sleeping near the pizza-lady house at night. At least I could tell Adam I wasn't lying about spending the weekend with another woman.

In between nights with Ms. Rocky Mountain Pie, I drove to the North trail on Friday morning. A Ford sat in the parking lot. Jake was doing his thing. Hopefully not his killing thing. I felt relief that he seemed to be carrying on as if nothing had changed.

I started to dial the Leadville Police Department number. I stopped, asking myself, "What would I tell them?"

"Uh, yeah, uh, there's a guy in town that might kill someone? The pizza lady has a nice rack, and I'm pretty sure I just saved her life."

I imagined the person on the other end of the line asking me if a crime had been committed. Had I been hurt? Had I been threatened?

"Uh, and Jake looked at me funny. Isn't that enough to go on?"

My mind crawled through a maze with no outlet. How was I going to stop this?

Tires made crunching noises as I pulled out of the gravel parking lot and onto a dirt road guided by Half Moon Creek. Mt. Elbert looked down its nose at me as the wind seemed to whisper in my ear: "Go home, pussy." I drove past a vacant campground and back toward town.

Later that night, as predictable as freezing temperatures in Leadville, I saw Jake's Mt. Elbert selfie. There he stood, wearing sunglasses and a proud smile. His face framed the edge of Twin Lakes shining in the distance. Later I saw a Facebook check-in of Jake at a bar in Boulder. As usual, Jake had more energy than me. He'd hiked Elbert then driven to the University of Colorado town to rest up for Saturday's football game. I considered following him there but for what purpose? He would be on full alert now. Nothing good could come from another interaction with him.

With Jake off to Boulder, I explored Leadville. The National Mining Hall of Fame was pretty cool. Interesting stuff, but I was too depressed and maybe a little too scared to get into it.

I bought a bottle of Jameson at the liquor store and replayed the chance meeting in my head over and over again. I felt drunk from lack of oxygen and sleep and let the whiskey pile on. I felt clueless. He obviously knew that I knew. I had no idea what he would do with this information. I would have to carefully line up all of my research and information and find a way to present it to police. The cops might laugh at me, I'd just have to nut up and take it. All while watching my back. He had to be concerned, but what did I actually have on him? Still nothing anyone would buy.

As I began noting everything, a terrible thought crossed my mind. Was he killing someone now while I was sitting on my ass? Another drink. There was nothing I could do about that now. I imagined the guilt I'd feel if a woman in Boulder disappeared tonight. His craving for killing had to be gnawing at his gut. He was going to hit again–soon. The weight of that thought added to the guilt I felt about misreading this guy so poorly. What had I missed with this guy when we were kids? How did I not see this coming? I thought about all the things we'd done as kids. We were mischievous at times. We had sling-shot a few birds. Egged a few houses. Did that make us future serial killers?

He was a total prick sometimes, but I couldn't remember him physically hurting anyone. Then an image came into focus. Not a predictor of murder perhaps, but something from his well of darkness.

Jake and I both played high school football. He was a decent athlete. He started at wide receiver for a team that threw the ball so rarely that it was essentially a trick play.

I played some linebacker, but was more like the Rudy Ruettiger of the team. I didn't have much athletic ability, but I played my ass off. Every play, including practice. I pissed off some guys from time to time when I leveled my own teammates.

I loved football, so much that we'd get some neighborhood games going from time to time in the spring. Tackle with no pads. I excelled in those neighborhood games, mainly because most of those kids didn't play real football. I felt like Walter Payton in that crowd. Like the skinniest boy at fat camp. Most of the guys playing were in the school band. And maybe not even the best football players in the band.

There was Ron, an oboe player who loved to talk trash despite his total lack of athleticism. And what the hell was the point of the oboe, anyway? Maybe the part in a movie soundtrack when a klutz walks into the room. That's it. Sam, a 6-foot-4 trombone player, who everyone thought should be a basketball player. Until they saw him play basketball. The triplets, who didn't look much alike when you got to know them. But, in 7th grade band it took me a week to figure out it wasn't one dude who could play three different instruments. Those were the regulars, though others showed up from time to time.

One spring Saturday, Jake joined us, saying he needed some exercise. I figured he wanted to put us all in our places by showing us what a real football player looked like. He wore a shirt with block letters that spelled out *Property of Mount Rainier Football* just to display what we already knew. A bandana signified that he was there to play.

Jake was the best athlete out there, but the no pads thing didn't suit him well. He also got a little lost on defense with every play being a pass play. We didn't really have what you'd call plays, but we played together so much that it seemed like it.

He covered me on defense, and I was holding up well. I kept crossing behind the other receivers to screen him off for little gains good enough for first downs. He was getting frustrated–he wasn't quite into it enough to fight through the screens and stop me. As I minimized his superior athleticism, his anger grew. The statement he'd hoped to make wasn't being read.

I liked that very much. I wasn't a smack-talker, but I did smile at him.

"Yeah, yeah, yeah," he said, face stuck in a scowl. "Big deal. Too bad you can't play real football worth a shit."

About halfway through the game, I caught a short pass. A teammate blocked him well and it turned into a long touchdown. I couldn't help myself–I laughed at him, a rare opportunity.

"Man, you're slower than I thought! Or am I just that damned fast!"

It felt great. So great it was pathetic. I was taking it to the guy who had essentially ditched me because I didn't quite fit his definition of cool. Including me in his group could only reduce his overall coolness score, and I wished they could all see this game. It felt good to rise above him, if only for a few minutes.

He was fuming.

I kicked off, aiming the ball straight at Jake hoping to drive home my point, whatever it was. He caught it and ran by two defenders. He juked a third, but came right into my sights. As he turned I blindsided him–hard. I'd never hit anyone that squarely in either real or neighborhood football. His head snapped forward over my shoulder, and his cleats lurched into my shins. His body took the shape of a horseshoe before flattening on the grass. I felt a joy equaled only by the births of my children.

Guys were snickering "Oh-ho-ho-ho-ho" the way guys do when they see a vicious hit. I popped up feeling about as badass as I've ever felt in my nondescript life. Jake gathered himself from the ground and started screaming.

"What the fuck is your fucking problem, you piece of shit? Do you think this is the fucking Super Bowl?"

He threw the football at me but missed, coming toward me as I marched at him. It took five guys to hold him back. One guy held me back, because I was more pretending to want to fight than actually coming at him. He twisted and turned, trying to shake the fleas off his hide. His eyes widened and looked like they'd pop out of his head. Rage. He'd completely lost his mind, and I had no doubt that he would have beaten the shit out of me if not for the guys screening him for me again, this time saving my ass.

After a few seconds of flailing, he relaxed a little, looking like a mental patient who'd just been administered a shot. His inferno turned into a slow burn.

"What a bunch of fucking scrubs. Total losers. You fuckers can play with yourselves."

He walked away, leaving us stunned. My exhilaration turned to slight sadness. He never played with us again, but at school it was as if nothing had ever happened. He resumed his spot atop the totem pole.

I hoped that would happen this time around as well. I just wanted things to go back to the way they were. Keep your top spot, Jake, and go back to ignoring me. The same way it's been for 30 years.

22

A GOOD KILLIN'

Leadville, Colorado

Jake facebook check-in: Dawgs are killing the Buffs! I love me a good killin'!–with Bob Peddin at Folsom Field, Boulder, CO.

That was as clear as the Leadville sky. The line was cheesy, even for him. He tagged me even though he knew I wasn't there just to make sure I got the message.

I love me a good killin'.

I went completely numb.

What now? I had to go to the police. Even if they thought I was crazy–and I was sure they would–at least they'd have somewhere to look if I disappeared after lifeless hike with Jake.

My only hope was that Jake would think I was too impotent to do anything with it. That he would get caught somehow before he felt the need to silence me. Or, maybe, he'd stop killing. Yeah, that's right! He knows he's being watched, and he'll simply stop killing people. Like the Green River Killer, who slowed his pace after being questioned by police. That irrational optimism faded quickly, and I'll admit I was fucking scared.

23

FREDO

Mallory Facebook post: I just watched The Godfather Part II again, and I hate to say it, but Fredo had it coming.

How cute, I thought at 35,000 feet on my way back to Seattle on Sunday afternoon. There were 21 likes and several comments. Except he hadn't watched it again, and it was the second threat aimed squarely at me. I was Fredo, the weak-minded brother that was going to betray him. Remind me not to go boat fishing any time soon.

I liked his post. I knew he'd notice that, and hoped he took it as threat received. Hey, how about we just forget about the whole thing and move on, Jake? I'll keep your secret. I won't betray you ala Fredo.

Thankfully, no Jake on the plane. That would have been awkward. *Hey, buddy, wasn't it funny how you were going to kill that lady and then I chased you back to town? Sure, pal, but I've got something even more hilarious in mind!* I guessed he flew back Saturday evening after the game. I wished I had, too, though not on the same plane.

Thankfully no one attempted to talk to me on this flight; otherwise, I might have become a murderer myself. A window seat this time, I sat next to what I guessed were sisters in their early 30s. The younger one featured a prettier face than her sister, but outweighed her by forty pounds. She wore baggy clothes, and I could relate to the desire for comfort and cover.

I felt like a dick for comparing the two, but that's the type of thing I do when I'm on a plane. Small spaces lead to big judgments.

The thin one offered her sister some mini-Snickers bars. Nice, I thought. Your younger sister already hates you for your body, and now you're trying to make matters worse.

"Oh, no thanks," she said, awkwardly.

A few minutes later, when her sister excused herself to visit the lavatory, she reached in her sibling's bag and quickly devoured two Snickers. I froze, not wanting my noticing to be noticed. I sipped my ginger ale and ate some pretzels to settle my uneasy stomach. I seriously considered testing my ability to drink on an airplane but decided against it.

It had been a quick flight. For some reason the flight home always seemed much faster to me. Clouds littered the sky as the plane neared Seattle. Mount Rainier poked through an opening to welcome me home, and I looked at it more intently than I had in years. It stood as a symbol of something else now. Another high point. Another potential burial ground.

We broke through the cloud cover and rain drops skittered off the wing outside my window. For the first time ever, it felt good to see rain. The Puget Sound stretched out to the Pacific Ocean, and I was happy to be on my way back toward sea level. I felt ready for some Great Living at 200 Feet.

The plane tires screeched on the runway, and soon I shuffled between rows of seats toward the exit. Though nervous to tell her about my fake trip, I so wanted Kathleen to be waiting for me when I exited the jet bridge. That's another thing that 9/11 took from us. The anticipation when you enter the terminal as your eyes search for your woman, your family, your kids, whoever is happy to see you. That smile, the hug, the makeout session if you're young and stupid. None of that for me. Whatever greeting I was getting this time would come at home.

"Hey buddy," a voice said from behind, sending a jolt of lightning through my chest. "You forget something?"

I turned around slowly, seeing a man pointing something in my direction. It was the scrap of paper I'd used to jot down some notes. It'd fallen out of my shorts pocket. I offered a meek "thanks," grabbed the piece of paper and headed for an exit.

I took the shuttle to the off-site parking area, and climbed in my Jeep. I desperately wanted to see Kathleen, but I dreaded the reunion a bit and lost my nerve. I was going to have to lie–a lot–about this trip. I would tell her about it all eventually, but now it was just going to anger and scare her. If she believed me. I decided it was best for her–and my own ass–to keep it to myself for a while. I didn't need her thinking there was a guy lurking in the cul de sac.

I hadn't called Kathleen once during the trip. Yeah, not a great husband move. She hadn't called me, either, just a couple of "how's it going" texts between us. Always great at giving me some space and likely busy with some rare girls nights while the husband and kids were in the care of others. Why bother talking to me? We would see each other soon enough. That's the type of trust and security we felt toward each other, at least until I threw that out the airplane window on the way to Colorado.

I felt anxious to get home but took my time. I had to gather my thoughts before I told her about my supposed trip to the UW game. The airport was not far from my old neighborhood, so I took a detour mostly because I couldn't think of another way to waste time.

I drove past my old house, a small, three-bedroom rambler I'd lived in until my mom's second marriage ended when I was a junior in high school. It was brown then, tan now. The little garden patch where my mom grew sunflowers in the front yard had been transformed back into overgrown lawn.

Seeing the house made me think about the dumb things I'd done in that house as a teenager. I'd tried smoking for the first time in that house. I'd stolen from the liquor cabinet and disguised the theft by adding water to the bottles. The first time I ever invited a girl to a house, it was that house. I'd planned to try to kiss her, but never got within three feet of her.

The neighborhood, which had been built in the '60s, was decaying. Plane traffic had increased, making that aspect of living in Des Moines stand out even more. People lived in this neighborhood because it was cheaper option in a region with exploding housing prices.

A plane flew overhead, and I remembered the windows rattling long ago when the old 727s roared across the sky. Most kids I knew could identify all the major jets by sight, and some by sound. Nothing roared quite like the 727, and it was easily identified without looking above.

I drove three blocks and stopped around the corner from Jake's house. It looked the same. The path I'd stealthily slinked along to raise him in the middle of the night to terrorize the neighborhood (or so we thought), bent around to the left. It didn't seem as though anyone was home. Perhaps he was flying back later today after all. I didn't move any closer for fear of being spotted, standing just around the corner. A couple of cars passed, drivers looking at me with curiosity. Yes, I'm a stalker. Move along, nothing to see here, folks.

The house itself was nothing special. But the perfect landscaping stood out in a neighborhood that had let itself go. I backed away and got back in my Jeep, wary of a run-in. We didn't need another car chase.

I retraced my old paper route–I was really stalling now. My memory had faded, but I could still pick out most of the houses where I'd used my quarterback skills. Seeing the neighborhood all these years later depressed me. I don't know if I'd built the area up in my mind over the years or if it was all fading fast. Everything seemed smaller and shittier, making it hard to understand why Jake stuck with it.

I stopped for a moment, viewing the house that brought back one of my worst newspaper quarterback moments. One large door and a small window had taken the place of a regular-size door and the 1960s orange textured window that I'd shattered years ago. I'd put a little too much on the throw, and the tightly-bound paper caught it just right.

I remembered walking gingerly up to the door. A black girl, a rare sight in the neighborhood back then, peered at me through the shards of glass that remained in the frame. She was beautiful–a couple of years older than me–and she looked at me sympathetically.

"I think the stupid dog broke the window," she said eyeing the wagging sheepdog who decided I was a new friend. She held him back so his paws wouldn't touch the broken glass.

"No, I..."

"Like I *said*, I think the dog broke the window."

She gave me a stern look, which slowly evaporated back to a perfect smile, her bright teeth shining like the moon.

I backed away and under-thanked her miserably before stumbling over a sidewalk lamp.

"Now, don't let the dog break that, too," she laughed.

I was scared shitless and in love. For the next year, I placed the newspaper squarely in the middle of the welcome mat at her house, lingering a few seconds longer than necessary. I never saw my guardian angel again and I certainly never had the balls to knock on the door. Part of me still thinks it was some sort of dream or hallucination.

I drove by Mount Rainier High School. They'd torn down the old one and built a beautiful new one that only made me feel ancient. I remembered the old covered walkways that gathered little raindrops and converted them into megadrops aimed at shooting down massive bangs girls wore back then.

I figured they soundproofed the new school. I thought again about 727s, which caused teachers to stop mid-sentence to wait for the building to stop rattling. My teenage years hadn't exactly been Fast Times at Mount Rainier High, but I suddenly missed the innocence of it all.

I pulled away from the school and began the short descent into downtown Des Moines. It was a little town bordered by Puget Sound that offered potential but never reached it. I drove past the pier where I'd walked with a girl or two and lost a footrace to my buddy Ray. I considered a stop at the old chowder house but kept driving. I was tired and scared of both the future and the line of crap I was going to have to sell at home.

I continued through town and followed Marine View Drive onto First Avenue and began the 45-minute drive home. Time to face normal life, I hoped.

I texted Kathleen about 15 minutes out, "Almost home, need anything?"

No response. Very unusual. Kathleen always had phone in hand, arm stretched out in front of her, giving her the look of a person in a permanent shoulder cast. Was she pissed? Maybe her damned phone died again. I kept reminding her that you can charge it before it completely dies, but it never quite sunk in.

I exited I-5 at Lynnwood and headed east, tires hissing along wet roads. Discount stores turned into houses, which grew bigger as I closed in on Mill Creek. I drove along Seattle Hill Road, which was once an old wagon road that connected Snohomish to Seattle long before suburbia sprouted around it like blackberry bushes. What would a farmer from 1885 think of this area now? Still not looking forward to the stories I would have to tell, I thanked the ridiculous 25-miles-per-hour speed limit, the one and only time, as my Jeep crawled along the tree-lined road.

I left the Mill Creek golf-course houses behind, closing in on the finish line at the end of my cul de sac. I noticed that Kathleen's SUV sat in the driveway next to an old Ford pickup that had belonged to my grandfather. I paused, took a deep breath and bounced my carry-on suitcase up the three stairs leading to the entryway of the house. The front door was open, an odd sight. She never left the door open, and rarely left it unlocked for more than five seconds. There had been many times when I had banged hard on the door, irritated that she'd gone into auto-lock mode when I'd simply gone out front to check the mail. She'd even sworn it wasn't her a few times, like it was a lock fairy.

To the left of the door, a broken window that wasn't the work of a paperboy.

Panic set in.

I dropped my baggage and bolted into the house. "Kathleen? Kathleen! Kathleen?"

Nothing. Deadville. Living room, kitchen, family room, laundry room. Nothing.

I ran into our bedroom. Drawers open, but no Kathleen.

Annie's room. Nothing.

I entered Mason's room, and saw a severed head on the floor, quickly realizing it wasn't real. Fucking Halloween.

I ran downstairs again. The living room was trashed. Broken glass from the china cabinet, everywhere. Overturned furniture. A broken coffee table.

A note, with letters cut from a magazine:

"Low point of your day: I've got her

Bring $25,000. You'll know where."

I fell to the floor and sobbed. How could I let this happen? It was time to call the police, something I should have done long ago.

"9-1-1, what's your emergency?"

"It's my wife," I sobbed, with a resigned tone. "She's been kidnapped."

"She's been kidnapped? Is that what you said, sir?"

"Yes, she's been kidnapped!" I shouted this time.

"Are you still in the house?"

"Yes, please send someone!"

"Is there anyone else in the house?"

"No, just me. No one else."

"Why do you believe your wife has been kidnapped?"

"The window was broken," I said, gasping for air, voice working itself into a fervor. "There's a ransom note. There's stuff broken everywhere. Her car is here but she's gone. She's gone! Please send someone NOW!"

"Sir, I'll dispatch someone immediately. What is your address?"

"I know who did it. Jake Mallory. Please send someone here, and have someone look for Jake Mallory. He lives on 20th Avenue South in Des Moines.

"What is *your* address?"

I gave the operator my address and waited. I didn't touch anything, well, any more than I had already. I'd seen enough cop shows and Dateline episodes to know better. I glanced at the note from afar. My heart raced and my eyes darted around the room, begging for a sign that would tell me she was OK.

I could see a Sports Illustrated magazine on the floor, the likely source of the letters. It was my magazine–a gift from my in-laws. I always had every intention of reading it but really got past the cover. Jake had now read more of it than I ever had.

Jake, I'm sure, thought this would be hilarious. What a silly way to kidnap my wife. A note right out of a Perry Mason episode. He took my wife and made it all seem like a big joke that only I would understand.

I wondered how long she had been gone. What was he doing to her? Where had he taken her? Was she even still alive? Anguish caused near paralysis as I considered my culpability. Why hadn't I rushed home the moment he figured out what I knew? I'd left her completely defenseless because I was too cheap to buy another plane ticket. I'd wasted valuable minutes driving around because I was too chicken-shit to go home. I felt physical pain in my stomach.

I texted my mother: "I will explain all of this later–you are just going to have to trust me. Kathleen has been kidnapped by someone I know. Jake Mallory. Please keep the kids safe. Do not answer the door. If he comes to your house call 911 immediately. Do not let the kids find out what's going on. Not yet."

"What? Are you kidding? I don't understand."

"Very serious. I'm sorry but I have to go."

It felt bad to send her something so blunt and out of the blue. She called. And called again. And again. I ignored it all. I had to focus and there was nothing I could do to calm her. I couldn't even calm myself. Seconds ticked away. I could feel her disappearing.

Four Snohomish County Sherriff's deputies, two ambulances and a fire truck arrived.

"Sir, are you injured?" asked one cop, signaling the other three to enter the house. He was the oldest of the three. He was a little over six feet tall and had developed a slight gut covered by a shirt that was now just a touch too tight. A coarse, reddish-brown, perfectly-groomed mustache hung over his lip.

"No," I answered. "There's no one else here."

"You did not see anyone else in the house?"

"No."

"What about the rest of the premises? Garage? Yard? Shed?"

"I didn't check any of those places."

I was already becoming impatient. You would think all my years of parenting, teaching and coaching would have forced me to become more patient. It hadn't. The one place I knew Kathleen wouldn't be found was in the garage. They were already wasting valuable time on top of what I had already wasted myself. A crippling pain hit my gut again, causing me to sway. My fault. All of it.

More police cars filled the cul de sac. Neighbors peaked through curtains. The next-door asshole, Old Man Hanks, came out to check his mail–it was Sunday and by no means did he miss it yesterday–while attempting to gauge the situation. Sadly, he might be my only hope. Maybe the nosy fucker had seen something.

I stood outside, impatience turning to anger. Every second they talked to me, the further Kathleen slipped away. I had nothing for them. I knew Jake wasn't dumb enough to leave anything behind, and anything they found would only be planted to throw them off the scent.

Two detectives found me outside.

"Hello, sir, I'm Detective Shane Stevens. This is Detective Andy Hanson. How are you holding up?"

How am I holding up? Stupid question. I disliked him immediately. The other one looked like he was dumb. Dopey. Except for the mustache, trimmed just a little too closely inside the corners of his mouth. It wasn't quite a Hitler 'stache but it made you look twice.

"Not well, detective. Have you found anything?"

"Sir, who is Jake Mallory?" he said, ignoring my question.

I hesitated. How much do I tell them? What could I say to get them to find him instead of thinking I was a nut job?

"It's a long story. He's an acquaintance, and I think he may have killed at least one woman. He knows I think this, and that's why he's got my wife."

I said it a little too loudly, like we were talking as a helicopter landed. They looked me over again, assessing my level of crazy.

I gave the cops a quick rundown. I figured out he'd killed people. I followed him to Colorado. He caught me following him and was taking it out on my wife. Simple as that. Find him and arrest him, please.

Here's something you should know about me. I can't stand it when people don't believe me. I'm not a bullshitter, and I hate wasting words. I believe everything I say has a purpose. People get mad at me because I think I'm always right. The truth is, when I talk, I usually am. I don't mean this to sound cocky. If I don't know something, I keep my mouth shut–an undervalued human trait. This means that I often come off as a stubborn ass. I will admit it when I'm wrong, but usually I don't open my mouth unless I'm pretty damned sure I'm right. Sadly, maybe that need to be sure of all this is what had kept me quiet so long. My need to be sure I was right had led to my wife's… I couldn't stand to finish the thought.

The detectives watched me, having to decide between me being crazy or a liar. Or they could buy this far-fetched story of mine. It appeared they weren't in the mood for far-fetched and with every second that they searched my home, not looking for Jake, I grew more and more surly. I paced, visibly annoyed.

Detective Stevens wore a neatly pressed, beige-colored shirt decorated by a black necktie and a department patch on his left sleeve. His olive-green pants were surrounded by a belt that included a revolver, handcuffs, a radio, pepper spray and a baton. A gold star shined brightly on his chest and daily-polished leather shoes glistened even in the drably-lit evening. Hanson wore all the same stuff, but it looked like he'd had it on for three days straight.

"Sir, when is the last time you saw your wife?" Stevens asked.

"I told you–before I left for Colorado! You've got to look into Jake Mallory. I know it was him."

"We'll check that out sir," Stevens said, dismissively.

I could feel the eyes of my neighbors. I'd treated them much like airplane seat neighbors. Not rudely, but unwelcoming. As few words as possible. With all the emergency vehicles outside, they knew some serious shit was going down.

"Sir, would you mind coming down to the station so we can go over a few things?"

I felt defeated as the seconds ticked away.

"Whatever will help," I said, forgetting every episode of Dateline I'd ever watched. "Let me grab my keys."

"Sir, we need to leave your car here–take a look at it in case there might be any evidence there."

"There's no evidence in my Jeep," I said. "She hasn't been in there for as long as I can remember and I just brought it back from the airport."

He nodded but without agreement.

Another lesson from this experience. Cops don't much like it when you appear to feel inconvenienced. An innocent man, of course, would welcome anything and everything the police deemed necessary to solve the crime. On the off chance there might be a clue up my ass, then I should be expected to bend over without protest.

No matter how much time they were wasting. No matter how much closer to death Kathleen became with each passing second.

"I understand, sir. We just need to rule it out."

Though not intentional, I threw every ounce of negative body language I had at them and got in the back of a Chevy Impala. It smelled of old cigarettes and Taco Bell. A roll bar outlined a steel divider between front and back seats, perforated at eye level to allow conversation. I looked at the shotgun standing straight up between the front seats, wishing I could point it at Jake's head.

The neighbors had to be loving the show. Facebook probably buzzed about it as well. My phone rattled repeatedly with text messages, mostly from people on the street that my son had played ball with at one time or another.

Paul: Hey bud evrything OK?

Steve: I hope all will be well. We are praying for you.

Robyn from around the corner: What's all the commotion on your street? You causing trouble again?

I read those only because I couldn't exit out of those and many other messages fast enough. No, I was not OK. And, thanks, Steve but God could not help me now–it was all up to Jake. I'd used up all my prayers for important things like outcomes of football games.

We reversed my earlier drive on the way to the Snohomish County Sherriff's Office South Precinct. It was located in downtown Mill Creek, across from the post office and a couple of blocks away from Mill Creek Town Center, one of those trendy lifestyle centers that continue to sprout all over the place. I was just glad this one didn't call itself "Towne Centre" like so many others in an effort to sound quaint.

We drove past the rain-soaked American and Washington flags flapping in the wind and entered the tan building, which seemed nondescript and small for a police station. I realized I hadn't been in a police station since that time Jake and I got picked up for rearranging reader board letters. I'm not sure what I expected. Maybe handcuffed punks wearing leather and spikes. A surprisingly witty prostitute trying to bargain her way out of trouble. An angry lieutenant barking orders and threatening to take the badges of cops who just flat-out refused to do things by the book.

No, none of that. None of anything on a Sunday night in Mill Creek.

We entered a tiny room. I'd always imagined a huge room with a low-hanging light and metal chairs that squeaked when they were moved. This seemed more like a school's time-out room with crappy office furniture.

"Mr. Peddin, are you OK with us recording this interview?"

"Yes, no problem."

I'd decided to put aside my anger toward the time we were all wasting and cooperate as fast as I could. Hopefully they'd get this over with and start really looking.

"I just want to make you aware that you are free to go at any time–we just want you to help us to figure out what happened. Normally, we'd wait a while to follow up, but with the house being, uh, disturbed…"

"I understand," I said, wondering why being free to go was even worth mentioning. Was I almost *not* free to go?

"Whatever I can do to help."

I took him through my day. Flew home. Drove home. Found the broken glass and the note. I left out the part about driving around. I'm not sure if it was because it made me look bad or because it was too painful for me to say out loud. Those valuable minutes… .

"Has anyone tried to find Jake Mallory?" I asked again.

"We're looking into that, sir. Were you and your wife having any marital issues?"

Oh. So that's where we were headed. It's always the husband…

24

SEARCH HISTORY

Mill Creek, Washington

Rhonda, annoying mom, Facebook post: "OMG, I hope Kathleen Peddin is OK. Its not like her to not be their for her kid's.

Detective Stevens was a little guy with a Napoleonic complex. He looked 20 at first glance, and when he talked sounded like a teen whose voice had just changed. A few wrinkles around the edges of his eyes gave him away as late 30s.

I'm guessing no one ever likes his interrogator. I was no exception. Stevens asked the questions he had to ask, often multiple times, perhaps in an effort to try to trap me. As I answered them, I could see his ice blue eyes already preparing the next question. He barely listened, seeming sure he already had all the answers.

I surrendered my phone so they could "rule some things out." They asked me where I'd been, and again I explained the timeline of my trip. I saw each repeated question as more seconds off Kathleen's clock.

"So, again, why did you go to Colorado?"

"I was afraid Jake Mallory might be going there to kill someone. I didn't..."

"Kill someone?" Stevens interrupted. "Why didn't you call the police?"

"Yeah, why didn't you call the police?" asked Detective Hanson, doing his best Lennie to Stevens' George. I eyed Hanson's mustache again. It would have been totally nondescript if Hitler hadn't been one of the most evil men in the history of humankind. How many people might be walking around with that look right now if not for Hitler?

Stevens looked at him and smirked, then looked back at me. I began explaining the whole Facebook, high points and murder thing, which was quickly becoming my Bermuda Triangle.

"You need to find Jake Mallory," I said again.

"Yeah, we're looking–we'll get a hold of Mallory."

He said it quickly, like a husband telling a wife he'd definitely fix the leaky dishwasher just as soon as he could.

"He has her," I said. "The words 'low point' in the note were meant for me."

We went through my theory again. Tick tock. They listened, but it didn't look like they were biting. Tick tock.

"Why would he ask for ransom?" Stevens asked.

"I think he just did that as sort of a joke," I said. "It's hard to explain."

"A lot of things are hard to explain," said Hanson, nose held high to be used as sights for a judgmental look.

Stevens, not liking Hanson's weak attempt at playing bad cop, glared at him with eyes that said, *Sarge promised me you wouldn't be allowed to talk when he made you my partner,* then turned his stare on me.

"I'm trying to help you here. But, there are a few things I don't understand. You said your flight landed at 3:50. But you didn't call us until 6:37. That's a lot of time. Where'd all that extra time go?"

"Well, I had to take a shuttle to pick up my car. I drove around for a while…"

"You drove around. You leave your wife and kids to go to Colorado, and instead of rushing back to see them, you drive around?"

Another punch in my gut. Not from the cop but from my own guilt. It hadn't happened the way these detectives believed, but there's no doubt I was responsible for all of this. Abandonment. Reckless endangerment. Call it what you want, this was my fault.

"I just, I just, needed some time," I answered defensively.

"Huh? Time to do what?" Hanson asked before a look of, *oh yeah, sorry, I forgot* formed on his bloated face in response to another Stevens' stare.

"Sir, you have any reason to harm your wife?"

"Absolutely not," I said, beginning to sob with the thought of what Jake might have done to her.

Stevens and Hanson left the room for a moment, then reentered. Later I would figure out that they were getting on-the-fly information from other cops who were going through my house, computers and phone while canvassing the neighborhood. They didn't exactly have the bloodhounds out looking for Jake.

"Mr. Peddin, was there another woman in the picture?"

"No, not at all."

"That's not what your friend Adam said."

Screwed. It's always the husband. Stevens let the question hang in the air while searching my reaction.

I glanced at my reflection in the one-way window and saw a future Dateline star. I turned back toward Stevens, whose smiling expression seemed to say "Busted." I couldn't find any words, so Stevens moved on to the next question.

"Let me ask you again, Bob," Stevens said, sternly. "Have you ever been physically abusive or intimidating toward your wife."

"No, never. I would never do anything like that."

It was true. We'd argued like any other married couples, probably less. Maybe raised our voices a few times. But I had never and would never put a hand on a woman. Or a man for that matter. I'd always felt like fighting was a sign of mental weakness.

"Have you ever threatened her? Screamed at her?"

"No, nothing like that. I would nev…" I said before Stevens cut me off.

"Then why were you overheard yelling, uh," Stevens paused and looked at his notebook for dramatic effect, before punctuating the next three words, "Die. Bitch. Die."

"I was…" I started, thinking about the mouse in my garage, the one I'd chased with a baseball bat while yelling those words, before I was interrupted again.

"Neighbors heard you scream 'die, bitch, die' and then heard crashing sounds."

"I, I," I stammered, getting nowhere.

He had me on the ropes and kept pounding me with what he'd learned, hoping for a cop's TKO: A confession.

"They've also heard you yell at your children. You called them pussies?" he said, having no interest at all that I'd been yelling at baseball officials through my television when I'd said that. "Who calls little kids pussies? That's just pathetic, Bob. That's terrible."

"Where is your wife Bob?" Stevens shouted.

My neighbor must have taken great pleasure in giving them the rundown. He probably considered poor yard maintenance to be a precursor to murder. I could hear him being interviewed by a news crew. *I always knew there was something suspicious about him.*

Stevens stood up.

"Where. Is. Your. Wife. Bob?" He pounded the back of his chair to accentuate each word. Not always a great intimidation tactic when you're 5-foot-5, but I was still scared shitless.

"I, I," I stammered again.

"You what?" he yelled. "What did you do, Bob?"

He moved close enough for me to smell coffee.

"What did you do to her?" he shouted, moving closer. "Kathleen. Your wife. The mother of your two children. What did you do to her, Bob? Things will be a whole lot easier if you just tell us now."

He drug out "ohhhh" part of the word "whole" so it sounded like the beginning of the SpongeBob SquarePants song.

"Where is she, Bob? Her family, the people who are worried sick deserve to know. Right now."

This is where I started to look like the dumbass husband whose brilliant plan to kill his wife and get away with it had failed miserably. Just like the dipshits on Dateline. I hesitated and stammered. I ducked my head and displayed child-like body language. I figured that if this video ever reached Dateline that even I'd think I appeared guilty if allowed to watch it from jail.

"I, I, I don't know. I don't know."

I sobbed, broken. I started to understand why false confessions happen. I just wanted to get out of that tiny room, but I said nothing.

Stevens, sensing he'd won Round 1 but that I was still standing, reeled it all back in. Hanson played with a hangnail.

"OK, take me back through this again," Stevens said, now trying to sound sympathetic.

Two hours later, I'd had enough. We'd gone through my story over and over again. Stevens left, and Hanson bumbled through a few questions. Then more Stevens. Then another detective. They were getting nowhere and neither was I. We were all frustrated, though for markedly different reasons.

"Am I still free to go?" I finally muttered, several hours later than I should have asked that question. The pain in my gut was gone now, replaced by sorrow and defeat.

"Yeah, you're free to go," said Stevens, giving me a cold look that reminded me of Robert Patrick playing the bad terminator in *Terminator 2*. "For now, you're free to go. For right now."

I knew that could change at any moment. I didn't even ask for my phone back, and had no interest in another squad car ride. I walked to Mill Creek Town Center and found what may have been the last pay phone on Earth. I had explained this novelty item to my kids recently. I called a cab. It was early on Monday morning, and cars taking their drivers to work began to appear.

Our house had been turned upside down. Search warrant. Computers and tablets gone. I could feel neighbors eyes upon me again as I paid the driver and trudged toward the front door.

After trying to sleep for an hour, I left the house to buy a new phone. I had to be able to access any method Jake might use for contact. A local mega-store opened at 7 a.m., and I purchased a new iPhone at full price–$799. I had no choice. My messages–voice, text, email and Facebook–had piled up like the contents of a Honey Bucket. I searched for anything from Jake, and found nothing. Jake had gone silent. No messages to me, and not one Facebook post or check-in.

I did the math in my head. If Jake's check-in at Folsom Field had been legit, it put him in Boulder at 1:15 p.m. on Saturday. The game started at 12:30, meaning it would end sometime around 4:00. After a 45-minute drive to Denver International Airport, he could easily catch a 6:00 flight.

He could have left earlier, but either way he probably didn't break into my house until at least 11 p.m. On a Sunday night, the neighborhood would be sound asleep. So, if he left my house by 1 a.m. Sunday morning, he could be, well, pretty much anywhere. Thirty hours had passed. If properly motivated, he could have driven 2,000 miles by now.

After driving home, I called Detective Stevens. Though I was Suspect No. 1, I had to make sure they were looking for Jake. I wanted to hide or maybe even curl up and die. But, I decided to keep bugging the cops.

"Have you found Jake Mallory?"

"Oh, hello Mr. Peddin," he answered, surprised to hear from me. "No, not yet. No answer at his residence or any of his phone numbers."

He said it like a teenager explaining to his parents that there would be no liquor or unsavory characters at the party he was planning to attend.

"Did you contact his employer?" I said, sounding like a parent asking if there would be adults at this party.

"We'll do that soon enough, Mr. Peddin." Aha. The teenager had not bothered to ask if the parents were home at this party he wanted to attend. This never makes a parent happy.

"Soon enough? What the fuck are you waiting for?"

"Hey, calm down, Mr. Peddin. We'll find him. In the meantime, could you come down to the station again? I just have a few more questions for you."

"He could be anywhere by now! You idiots are wasting your time with me while he's taking her to God only knows where!"

"Bob," he said before I interrupted him by shouting "Fuck!" into phone.

"Bob," he said undeterred. "Could you please come down to the station?"

At this point, I wanted to do what an innocent man does–try to help the police. Without the slightest clue where Jake had taken my wife, I also had nothing else to do at the moment. Going to see the cops is a great idea as long as you're not the suspect. There's a difference between knowing you're innocent and the cops believing it.

As I walked out the front door, my new phone rang: Kathleen's mother. I couldn't even begin to think of what I'd say to her. A good husband would have figured out something to make this poor, suffering woman feel a little better. But, I ignored the call. I had one purpose in life–to find Kathleen or get the cops to find her. Nothing else mattered. Not what the cops believed. Not Kathleen's mother's fear. Not whatever people were saying on Facebook about Kathleen's horror story.

My second interview with Stevens didn't last long. He explained to me that there was no trace of Kathleen. No credit card or phone use. No one had seen her since the night before. Nothing.

"First off, Mr. Peddin, I just got a call from Kathleen's mother. Apparently you are not answering her calls?"

I stared blankly at Stevens. I knew this looked bad. Really bad. A guilty man ignores the mother-in-law. By now I had resigned all hope that he would believe me, and as long as he didn't place me under arrest I really didn't give a damn.

"I just haven't had a chance to call her back."

"You didn't have time to call her back," he said, volume of his voice increasing. "The mother of your missing wife. A mom who's scared to death about her daughter and cried herself to sleep. You didn't have time."

He shook his head in disgust. Part real, part act.

"I know, I should have called her back. I'm just trying to stay focused on helping you find Kathleen."

I don't know why, but when I said that it sounded rehearsed. Like a part of a prepared statement. I expected him to continue making me feel like the worst son-in-law in the world, but he came at me from a new angle.

"So, who is the other woman?" Stevens asked.

"There isn't another woman."

We had discussed this already during the first interrogation, and I was in no mood to continue.

"Come on, Bob," he said, with a you-can't-bullshit-a-bullshitter smile. "Who's the other woman?"

"There isn't another woman."

"OK, then help me understand why you asked your friend to cover for you if your wife called. You told him to say to your wife that you were with him, but you were really having an affair. That doesn't look good, Bob."

He smiled at me now with mock sympathy. *Shucks, Bob, too bad your dick's going to get you killed. Bummer, man…*

"Hey, I get it, man. You'd been together for a long time. It's only natural to get a little bored and start looking."

"That's not what happened."

"You meet another woman, and it's all innocent enough," he shrugged. "Then things start to happen. You get close and realize the new woman's the one you want to be with. But, what do you do about your wife?"

"I lied to Adam," I said, somehow waking up Hanson.

"Oh, you lied!" said Hanson, pretending to be shocked. "You've done a lot of lying lately, haven't you Bob?"

Remembering his place, Hanson ducked his head down before Stevens could smack it.

"I lied because I didn't want her to know I was following Jake Mallory. I just didn't want her to worry."

"Oh, right, Jake Mallory," Stevens said, with a calculated eye roll.

I'd been calm, but this made my insides burn. He decided to switch gears.

"One other thing. Have you maybe used the internet to figure out ways to kill a woman and get away with it?"

He asked this in an almost falsetto voice, the one you might use to accuse a 5-year-old of sneaking a cookie before dinner. Stevens enjoyed himself. His body language and tone, I guessed, had been practiced in the mirror. He was good cop, bad cop, sympathetic cop, judgmental cop and brother cop all in a span of five sentences. An asshole of all trades.

"No," I said, calmly, knowing where he was going with his questions.

"So, can you explain why your computer was used to search for missing mothers, human butchering and other things related to the death of women? That's pretty sick shit, Bob. I won't lie–some of the sickest shit I've ever seen. And, I've seen a lot of sick shit."

I thought about the articles I'd searched about dead women. And worse. I'd looked up decomposition rates. How hard it was to chop up bodies. Large hiking backpacks. This was not going to end well for me.

"You've got this all wrong, detective. Please, please find Jake Mallory," I said, emotions starting to burble again. I thought about Kathleen and started to sob again.

Stevens offered a knowing look to Hanson, which seemed to say, *nice try with the crying*. Hanson stared at a stain on his shirt and missed it.

Tears of anger and frustration trumped tears of fear and sadness. As these clowns stuck to the Husband-Always-Does-It playbook, Jake was running wild on another playfield. I thought of a high school running back I'd seen play a few years earlier. He was a great runner, but what really beat the other team was his ability to make it look like he was the one with the ball when he actually didn't. He was so good at finishing the fake that the defense would tackle him and a referee would blow the whistle–all while a wingback ran the other way untouched. Jake was the wingback, and these cop refs were blowing the play dead. I was the only one who could stop it. The only one who could find Kathleen. How, I had no idea.

One thing I knew: We were not getting any closer to Kathleen in that interrogation room.

"Look, I hate to do this, but I guess I'm going to need a lawyer if there are any more questions," I sighed. "I really don't know anything. You've got to find Jake Mallory. He has her, and you're wasting valuable time on me."

I said it half-heartedly. I was no longer trying to convince them. I felt defeated. Stevens and Hanson would never really take a look at Jake. I was their guy, and all they had to do was finish the tackle. My only play was to stay on my feet long enough for something miraculous to happen. I needed a Doug Flutie Hail Mary, or a running-through-the-Stanford-Band type of play. The problem, though, is that desperation plays fail almost all of the time.

"OK, Bob, if that's the way you want to play it," Stevens said, disgusted. "You're free to go, for now. Don't go far, though. You'll be back in here soon, and next time you won't be going home."

I walked out of the station and pulled out my phone. Suddenly, I knew where I was going, and it wasn't home.

PART III
BAD ALTITUDES

25

STRANGE BREW

Albuquerque, New Mexico

Jake Facebook check-in: I knew I should have taken that left turn—at Albuquerque, New Mexico.

I "liked" the check-in.

I've never felt so alone. There was not one person I could talk to right now who would believe me. Everyone figured me for a nut, a wife-killer or both.

My mind would wander, thinking about what might be happening to Kathleen right now. If she was still… .

No time for negative thoughts or for my imagination. I had to focus. I booked the next flight out that I could make. The price hurt: $952. I felt guilt for thinking about money at a time like this.

As I drove to the airport my mind wandered again, this time to Mason and Annie. Would they be motherless? Fatherless?

I hadn't bothered to contact my own mother after the text I sent moments after walking into my house-turned-crime scene. The kids were supposed to come back today, and I hoped they hadn't heard anything to make them worry. I wondered what would be worse. Two dead parents, or one dead and one in jail? I decided it's probably better for both parents to be dead if you thought the father died trying to save the mother. If your father was in jail for killing your mother–no shrink could cure that shit.

I parked my Jeep in the airport garage and jogged to airport security. I've never seen a line so long. It snaked through the concourse, down some stairs, and snaked some more. I panicked at the thought of missing my flight, but knew causing a scene would not end well. Hell, my mug shot might be on the news by now.

The line moved more quickly than expected and I reached the gate with time to spare. Benches with rounded butt holders to make them almost seem like individual seats were filled with people just close enough together that you'd be a total asshole if you sat down between them. I stood, fidgeting like a kid waiting for the dismissal bell.

Once again, I considered calling the police, though this time it would be the Albuquerque police. I thought about all the times I should have called the police over the past few months, and could no longer think of valid reasons for not at least trying. Kathleen would tell you it's because I'm a stubborn asshole. There's definitely some truth to that.

I also came from a family that insisted each member try to figure out his or her own shit. *Oh, you want dinner? I'll show you how to cook so you don't have to ask tomorrow. Need a clean pair of socks? You bet, kiddo, here's the washing machine–it will guarantee you clean socks for life if you're willing to get off your ass.* I never thought this was a bad thing. I remember going to a friend's house when I was about 8 years old. We wanted some lunch, and he was waiting on mom to make us PB&J sandwiches. She was busy, and kept giving him the *just one more minute* routine for a good hour.

"Why don't we just make them ourselves?" I asked.

He looked at me like I'd suggested we make our own rocket and eat green cheese on the moon. I felt sorry for him. Poor bastard couldn't even make a sandwich. I felt gratitude toward Mom that day, well, until she handed me a needle and thread that evening so I could sew my own damned patch onto my own damned holey jeans.

Beyond all that, I just hate asking people for help. There's a combination of not wanting to bother another person and not allowing them to think I'm a pathetic loser who can't handle a simple task.

It's an admission of weakness. So, yeah, I'm the guy who would never ask for directions. I'm the teacher who never, ever, ever talked to a parent or the principal to deal with student behavior–somewhere, I could hear my mother say, *Why do you need a principal to handle this for you? Can't you just do it yourself? Here, I'll show you this ONE time.*

Looking back, that's why I didn't go to the police in any of the states where Jake had killed or might soon kill people. It was the intersection of my two biggest fears–people not listening to me and people thinking I was a useless putz. *Can't you just stop this murderer yourself? Why do you need to bother someone else with this?* That inability to ask for help before going on this trip revealed my true weakness.

Now I was getting on this plane that was going to be the death of me one way or another. Either the plane was going to crash, or I was going to crash and burn at some point after it landed. Or, maybe, I would return home with nothing and wait for prison guards to escort me to the lethal injection room.

I found my seat on the 737, relieved momentarily that the one next to it was unoccupied. Given my state of mind, I would have almost paid another $952 to sit next to an empty seat. More people entered the plane, and I began evaluating my potential armrest partners. Three that had potential walked past my row. Maybe I'd have an open seat next to me after all.

Then, a woman in her 30s boarded the plane with her parents in tow. They were loud. The passengers suddenly became like-minded: Please not next to me. You could almost hear a synchronized chant. I hoped they had boarded the wrong plane. Or at least let them sit next to each other in another area, some secret, undiscovered soundproofed section of the jet.

They stopped at my row.

"OK, we've got one here, one there, and one over there," the daughter said, pointing out empty seats next to defeated passengers. "OK, Mami, you go there. And, Papi, why don't you sit next to this nice gentleman."

Ah, if she only knew she was putting her Papi next to a suspected killer. Today no one in Mill Creek was using "nice" or "gentleman" and my name in the same sentence unless "used to be" or "seemed like" was mixed in there somewhere.

Headphones in, I didn't acknowledge her compliment. Papi sat next to me, and whipped out a meal he'd purchased from Panda Express in the airport. Papi slurped at his Chow Mein, battling hard to keep it on his plastic fork long enough to deliver it to his mouth. Elbows flew wildly, like a center securing a rebound under the basketball hoop.

After a bone-on-bone shot to my elbow, I couldn't help myself. I gave him a dirty look. I might as well have sent him an invitation to my airplane party. Dirty looks are supposed to turn people away, but somehow they are often misinterpreted as a hello.

"Oh, sorry about that," he offered. "They don't give us much room in these metal tubes, do they?"

I offered a half-smile.

"Papi?" his wife asked. "Save some for me!"

This led to a couple of conversations for all of us to hear. *Why didn't you get your own damned food? Because I wasn't hungry then. How long is the flight? What's the temperature in Albuquerque?*

Blah-fucking-blah-blah-blah. If I was going to die on this trip, I wished it would just happen then so I wouldn't have to suffer a side show with Papi and Mami.

Interrupted by the beverage cart, I felt relief when their conversation lulled about 30 minutes into the flight.

I took a sip of my ginger ale.

"Ginger ale, huh?"

Great, maybe ginger ale was going to get someone killed after all.

"Yeah, ginger ale."

Papi stared at me blankly, expecting some sort of explanation for my beverage choice. As usual, I disappointed and began turning away.

"Usually a fellow puts something else in his ginger ale, if you know what I mean."

He raised his eyebrows three times in a way that is usually associated with something sexual. I considered saying: "I'd never put my penis in ginger ale," but let it go.

"A little whiskey goes great in there," he offered, nodding.

I offered a quick nod in response and started turning back toward my tray table.

Papi, however, asked a few more questions. Now, normally, I'd play along. I'd be annoyed, but once trapped, I'd be polite enough to make the person think I wasn't picturing them being sucked through the window and into the engine turbine.

"So, what takes you to Albuquerque?" he asked.

"Well, Papi," I said, looking straight into his eyes, speaking slowly, and too loudly for our close quarters. "A serial killer kidnapped my wife. She's probably dead. And, soon, I'll probably be dead, too."

Papi's eyes searched mine. I pictured a toilet overflowing inside his head.

"Oh. Uh, oh," was all he could muster.

I looked around with an "*Anyone else*?" look on my face and eavesdropping heads quickly turned away. It was pretty quiet after that.

I dozed off for about 20 minutes, dreaming that I was being interviewed by Keith Morrison.

"You've contended all along, that this is the work of a serial killer?" said, Keith with a straight face.

"Yes," I said, wearing bright orange with my arms and legs shackled.

"Cops have the wrong guy." Morrison said, eyebrows raised above his bangs, finishing my sentence for me. Keith putting words in the husband's mouth always made them look guilty.

"Funny thing about time," said, Keith now narrating over camera shots of the Des Moines Marina. "It flies–far out of one's grasp when a suspect can't explain why some of it is missing." Nice shot of a seagull flying across the sun, which was escaping the grasp of a cumulus cloud.

Thankfully, Papi's wayward elbow awakened me before Keith made me feel like total shit. The plane began its descent, and I looked down at New Mexico, a world in sepia tones.

On the ground, I took my phone out of airplane mode, and it lit up with multiple messages. I held my phone away from me like I was moving a wasp's nest, stung only by a couple of messages.

Jason, my best friend from college: Where are you man? Everyone's looking for you. If you need someone to talk to you've got my number.

Detective Stevens: Bob, please call me ASAP.

I exited the rest without reading them. Nothing from Jake since the Albuquerque post. I vowed not to check anything but his page until this was over. Wasted emotion leads to fractured focus. I cared about nothing but Kathleen, and of course Jake. Nothing else mattered, though the three missed calls from the sheriff's office rattled me momentarily.

I ignored it all. There was not a damned thing I could do for anyone, nor was there a damned thing anyone could do for me.

I exited the plane and followed the maroon and brown tiled floor toward the rental car shuttle. I passed all the typical Airport shops, including the ones that pretend to be local. In Seattle a store with miniature Space Needles and smoked salmon. In New Mexico, a combination of Spanish, Native American and Cowboy. And, of course, a Panda Express. I probably still had some on my elbow.

I checked Facebook again, and my next destination came into focus thanks to Jake's check-in:

Jake Mallory was at Nexus Brewery.

Nexus. I began overanalyzing, remembering the definition as a connection or connected group. Was this some sort of message?

I climbed in my rented Ford Explorer–I went bigger this time just in case–and suctioned an old GPS to the window. Like everything else I had with me, it was still packed from the Colorado trip. I knew mountains could be coming, and I couldn't rely on the usual phone navigation apps.

I took I-25 North, crossing I-40 at "The Big I" freeway interchange and exited at Pan American Frontage Road. My eyes danced at every intersection. I didn't know what I was looking for. It's not like they'd be standing on the side of the road waving me in with orange wands.

I fantasized for a moment that this was all a joke. Wouldn't this be an amazing prank? The greatest practical joke of all time. Hey, Bob, come on in and have a beer with us, sucker! I'd be willing to overlook the months of misery and expense to be the butt of a joke right now, I thought.

Two more right turns and I was at Nexus. A small sign read, "It's not just a place, it's an exBEERience. Gross, I thought. But, not gross enough to turn people away. Big crowd for a weekday, meaning they likely served good beer along with the bad puns.

I walked in slowly, eyes moving quickly, dissecting every living creature in the place. Thirty-somethings taking advantage of the tail end of happy hour took up most of the seats. Buddies having a couple after work. A business meeting or two. A casual, *Hey let's grab a beer sometime* date.

"You can go ahead and seat yourself," a waitress said without slowing her pace while balancing pints on a plastic tray.

"I've got this one," I heard a man's voice say to the waitress, who needed only two steps to forget my existence.

I turned to the voice, and saw a smiling man in his early 40s, offering a pint of brown liquid like it was a jewelry box.

"Mr. Peddin?" he asked more than said as he slipped into his pocket what just might have been a copy of my Facebook profile photo.

No, it wasn't Jake. I'd never seen this man before, but he grinned and looked at me with recognition.

"Uh, yeah."

"For you, sir. Slow Down Brown," he said offering me the pint of beer. "Compliments of Mr. Dave Hoffmann."

I was confused for a moment, before remembering that Dave Hoffmann, a linebacker for the 1991 University of Washington National Championship football team, was one of my favorite players of all time. Ah, good old Jake was making a funny again!

"Great, thanks. Is Mr. Hoffmann still here?"

"No, he said he was sorry, but he had another appointment and he would be in touch very soon."

My eyes continued to search. Beer bottles rested neatly along the top edge of the dark wall. An old Olympia Beer sign hung on the opposite wall, an odd sight considering that Olympia had been a brewery in Washington state. Olympia beer is still available, but it's brewed in California and owned by a Russian conglomerate. No one in Olympia drinks Olympia beer any more. Two men played pool on the table in front of the sign, sipping on pint glasses as they strategized.

"Was anyone with Mr. Hoffmann?" I asked.

"No, not that I saw."

"Are you sure–no woman with him?"

"No, sir, I never saw him with anyone."

I felt a pain in my chest. Did this mean she was dead already? If she was alive, where was he keeping her?

"Oh, and he was very explicit about this part: He said to enjoy the Slow Down."

"Now what?" I thought. Slow Down was some sort of message. Did he mean, ha ha, I'm slowing you down so I have time to kill your wife while you sit on your fat ass drinking beer? Or, did he mean, slow down, I'll tell you what's next? I decided to wait a few minutes. If I didn't hear anything, I'd start the drive to Wheeler Peak, which was the highest point in New Mexico. I had a feeling that's where we were headed. Then again, maybe not. He could just be toying with me before killing us both. I shivered as I remembered that sometimes his killings happen nearby but not at the high point. I had no idea where we were headed but figured he had a well-thought-out plan.

Beer was a bad idea, but I couldn't help a few sips. It was good beer, and felt great going down.

I read the back story to Nexus Brewing to pass the time. The owner's idea was to have a place where all types of people could meet and hang out together. A great idea, though I wasn't sure he envisioned hanging out with serial killers and murder suspects.

26

No Fucking Chance

Albuquerque, New Mexico

Mallory Facebook check-in: Waiting for a friend–at La Cumbre Brewing Company

Nice touch, Jake. La Cumbre, Spanish for "the peak." I jogged out of Nexus, pulling up La Cumbre on my phone. It wasn't far. I took a left on Montgomery, then drove a mile down Carlisle Boulevard and a half-mile on Candelaria. La Cumbre, nestled amongst warehouses, had a small parking lot that was full. Apparently Albuquerque likes its beer. I circled back and parked on the street in front of a heating and air conditioning place.

La Cumbre bustled. People walked between the brewery and the barbeque truck that sat out front. A haze hung in the air above the sidewalk fueled by sizzling meat and bar patrons who had stepped out for a smoke or a vape during the last few moments of dusk.

I speed-walked into La Cumbre, my eyes searchlights in the darkened room.

"Hey, man," said a nervous voice off to my side.

He was holding a pint close to his heart, like a baby.

"Um, are you Mr. Peddin?" he asked, as I noticed a small headshot of me between his fingers.

The tall but awkward man in his mid-20s shuffled a step closer. He dipped his head a bit, still hoping to be shorter. He wore John Lennon glasses and a collared black shirt.

"Yeah, that's me," I sighed. A look of relief took over his face. I hoped he'd been tipped well, as this clearly stressed him.

"A guy named Donald Jones bought this for you," he said, presenting me with my prize. "North Peak Porter."

Donald Jones. Hoffmann's UW football teammate.

"Thank you. Did, uh, Mr. Jones say anything else?"

"He said he was sorry he missed you, but that he'd be in touch. Oh, and enjoy the North Peak."

I checked Facebook (nothing new), and took a sip. Good stuff. I could see what was going on now. Obviously, Jake was fucking with my head. But, there was more to it than that. He was sending me little messages in a bottle, or rather, pint glasses.

So far, it seemed that we'd all be meeting on the north side of Wheeler Peak. But, not today. Slow down. Not yet. He was going to milk this one.

I thought of the police again. My imaginary conversations with them seemed to change a little each time. *Hey, police, this guy is checking in at brewpubs and buying me beer! Arrest him immediately! Who am I, you ask? Why, I'm a suspected murderer!*

I took a long gulp of my beer, which was halfway gone. My eyes wandered away from the heavy dark-brown liquid and toward a window, drawn there by that sense you get when someone is looking at you. In this case, staring.

I stood slowly, and the shadowy figure vanished. I moved toward the door as quickly as my body would allow, dodging bewildered beer drinkers. As I emerged from the building, I could see a man running down the street. I accelerated again, running into an old man in a Bitch Creek ESB shirt who was eating a brisket sandwich. He bobbled his meal twice before it fell to the cement.

"Hey, asshole!" he shouted over laughter from his buddies. "You better replace that."

We sprinted past where I'd parked, and two blocks later I saw him turn left into an alley separating two warehouses. I rounded the corner in time to see him cut right behind a darkened building. As I turned the corner I ran straight into Jake's elbow. He connected just above my left eye, knocking me off my feet so hard that the back of my head hit the pavement. As I tried to find my feet, I heard his footsteps pick up speed.

I worked at pulling myself off the ground, like a boxer trying to beat the 10-second count. I was already gassed even before the blow to the head. Sensing I wasn't going to catch him, Jake stopped at the intersection of a darkened alley. He wore a gray sweatshirt, black sweat pants and a black baseball hat. Like at Rocky Mountain Pie, he was dressed to be forgettable.

"You've got no chance against me, you piece of shit," he said through gritted teeth. "No fucking chance."

I looked around and considered calling for help. No use. La Cumbre was the only thing happening at night in that section of town and those people were blocks away.

"Just, just let her go," I stammered. "You're right, man, I've got no shot against you. We can just keep all this between us. There's no need for you to hurt her."

I considered my options. Jake had always been faster than me, and given our physical conditions 25 years later, that gap certainly hadn't shrunk.

"You never know, asshole," he said, a smile growing. "You just might get lucky and find her."

He cut west down another alley. Head throbbing, I stumbled after him, but he was right. I had no chance against him. I heard a car start and speed away on Vassar Drive, but I wasn't even close enough to see it.

27

Follow That Car

Albuquerque, New Mexico

Mallory Facebook check-in: Life would be a lot easier if they had one of these for Wheeler Peak.–at Sandia Peak Tramway.

Lump on my head, I'd checked into a hotel near La Cumbre shortly after my overly direct meeting with Jake. I set an alarm for every 30 minutes to look for Facebook check-ins from Jake. Also, I was told as a kid that it's a good idea to wake up every half-hour when you have a concussion.

Several hours before the Sandia Peak check-in, a sudden loud noise startled me at 3 a.m. I jumped to my feet ready to take on the shouting voice coming from inside my room. Just as quickly, I relaxed. The asshole who'd had the room the night before had set the alarm clock. I'm sure he'd be disappointed if he knew I was already awake. My pulse slowed enough to stave off a heart attack but not enough to avoid restlessness.

My phone buzzed occasionally. Both Kathleen's mom and my mom worried. The cops wanted to talk to me again. It seemed nothing had changed back home. Helpless, clueless, I sat on my ass while he was doing who knows what to my wife.

I couldn't stand the thought of life without Kathleen. To some, it may seem like we're disconnected. We have different interests and not much overlap in our friendships. At times, it almost seemed like we were just roommates. Or business partners. But, underneath all that was a deep love.

I felt like shit for not saying that to her. I was pretty sure she knew it, but I should have said it more. I thought back to freshman year of college. I met her in a dorm at the UW. McMahon Hall, which was a few bars short of being a penitentiary.

I was in a dark place at that time. Unsure of who I was or wanted to be and certainly no clue which direction I was heading. She brought some color into my world and made each day a little better. I was sure I wouldn't be alive now if I hadn't met her. I fucking owed her.

I had to figure this out.

Then, at 8 a.m. I saw that check-in. Sandia Peak? I liked the post, something I regretted later. His check-in didn't make much sense. This was perhaps the most popular tourist destination in Albuquerque. Even in the fall, I guessed it was heavily used. He couldn't take Kathleen up there. And, if he wanted to kill me, Sandia Peak wouldn't be the place.

I ran my fingers through my hair out of habit, took a piss and headed for the elevator. The doors opened, revealing an elderly couple headed for a morning swim in the pool. I smiled to be polite.

"Hello," the old man said.

"Gosh, what happened to your eye?" asked his wife.

"Scorpion got me," I answered as the doors opened.

I jumped in the Explorer and moments later accelerated onto I-25 North. I was ready for anything. Except traffic. I turned on the radio. There was some sort of major construction going on along Paseo Del Norte, a major highway that intersected with I-25. This was carmageddon. I got off I-25. The female voice in my GPS recalculated repeatedly, sounding annoyed. I finally settled onto Academy Road, then hit 556 North to Tramway Road.

With Sandia Peak looking down on me, I pulled into the paved parking lot. Preparing for a quick exit, I backed into a spot, remembering how much I hate getting stuck behind drivers who pull in backwards. They seem to always need 3 shots at it and still end up taking part of the next stall.

I walked up the stairs to the tram, half expecting someone to bring me a beer. A little early, I thought, but I could use one to calm my nerves. I wasn't a big fan of heights. Or kidnapping. Or death.

There was a sizable line for the trip up the mountain, but I got on the next one since I was probably the only person there alone. The tram filled up with couples, and a few extended families. While there was no school in Washington state today–some sort of teacher enrichment day that only the annoying teachers utilized while the rest of us slept–I guessed there must be school everywhere else. There were no children on this trip.

We began our ascent, and I looked at the cables holding all of us above the rocks. I wondered how often they checked them. They looked pretty freaking thin to me.

A teenager who sounded like Beavis (or was it Butthead?) served as our tour guide and told us all about the tram, pointing out landmarks along the way. It was a 2.7-mile trip that would take about 15 minutes. The views were breathtaking. This whole thing was supported by only two towers along the way, making me wonder why this thing hadn't fallen yet. I was pretty sure it was just a matter of time and thought it might be just the day for it.

What masochists decided to build something like this? A-ha. Skiers, our guide explained. Only crazy ideas come from skiers.

Somehow, ponderosa pine trees, some of them 100 feet tall, sprouted from the granite. I was skeptical. They looked a lot smaller from the car, a thought that made me shiver again.

Beavis told us we'd be passing the other car soon. Four cables ran parallel to each other, two used for each car. According to our guide, it was a double reversible jigback aerial tramway. Two cars ran opposite of each other. When one reached the top, the other reached the bottom.

"Be sure to wave at the folks in the other car," the teen said, attempting enthusiasm but falling well short.

I looked in the other car as it neared, and froze. Was that Jake?

The tram came closer and I pushed my way toward the window facing it, getting rude looks from the people in the car. After fighting my way through, I saw him again, just in time for him to flash a maniacal smile along with a throat-slashing gesture as his car grew smaller.

"Stop the tram!" I screamed.

People gasped. The teen, as if awakened from a nap said, "Whuh-what?"

"Stop the fucking tram! Now!"

"Sir, calm down," he said, almost whining.

"Fuck" I said, putting my head in my hands while realizing it made no sense to stop the tram anyway. What was I going to do, climb to the other car?

"Fuck, fuck, fuck," I whimpered.

My tram-mates were staring at me like I had Ebola and they were going to catch it. They probably wondered if I was a nutjob that was going to throw them all out onto the rocks. Panic does not play well in a tram. The bump on my head throbbed, and I could feel people staring at it.

"Sir, I can't stop the tram," the guide said.

"Are you OK?" a man a few years older than me asked, assessing the situation. I didn't look up at him, instead staring at his white New Balance walking shoes and white socks pulled tightly over his calf muscles.

"I'm, I'm sorry," I said, with my head down like a kid in a corner wearing a dunce cap. "I'm, I'm fine. I'm sorry. I'm really sorry."

"OK, folks, we're about to pass the second tower, as you can see…" Beavis rambled, back on track.

I stood looking out the window, the other 20 people in the tram giving me as much space as they could without breaking through the tram's glass. I didn't look at any of them, knowing I wouldn't be able to stand the looks on their faces. A few minutes later, we approached the top. They all exited, leaving me with nervous, sideways glances on the way out. Another group entered, pausing as they wondered why I hadn't disembarked to look around.

The teen eyed me, trying to decide if I was going to cause him any more grief. I wasn't.

"Are you, like, OK man?" he asked.

"Yeah, sorry about that."

"What, like, happened to your head?"

Poor timing for a typically innocent question. There are times when a person shouldn't ask a question if they don't know the answer. For example, it's a bad idea to ask a guy why he shaved his head if he just underwent chemotherapy. As I learned recently, you shouldn't ask about someone's mother if there's a chance she's dead.

"I hit it falling out of a fucking tram," I said, ending our conversation.

A few minutes later, the tram slinked back down the mountain as I seethed. He had been 10 feet away from me, but it might as well have been 10 miles. With a 20-minute head start, he would be long gone by the time I got back down there. Unless he had another elbow waiting for me.

The tram and the teen hummed along, both on autopilot, both moving on from the momentary drama I'd caused. Wind gusts occasionally rattled the windows, and the tram swayed as we crossed a tower that had been, according to Beavis, installed using helicopters. Our guide also pointed out a rock formation that looked like a dude wearing a turban. I didn't see it, though my search was as half-hearted as his description.

The tram sank down the lower section of the mountain along with my heart. The first two Facebook check-ins seemed to have a message. I wondered what it was supposed to be this time before deciding it was just a simple statement: I have your wife, and I own your ass.

Back in the Explorer, I sat paralyzed by indecision. Should I go to Wheeler Peak? Start canvassing brewpubs? Instead I waited for the next Facebook check-in to guide me.

28

PLEASE DON'T STAND SO CLOSE TO ME

Mill Creek, Washington

Dick Wallin Facebook post: Has anyone heard from Bob Peddin? No one can reach him and I'm concerned.

22 people reacted to this

Larry Rosenberger: I was just thinking the same thing. I hope they are both OK.

Sonja Welch: I heard the police are looking for him…

Rhonda Corwin: I started thinking about that last night. I cant believe whats happening to the Peddin's.

Ray McLeod: If I know Bob, he's out there trying to find her.

Sonja Welch: Uh, where's he looking? Seems like he'd be searching with the rest of us…

Dick Wallin: Thanks, everyone. Please let me know if anyone sees or hears from him. I'm afraid he thinks he knows who might have taken Kathleen and that he might be acting on it alone. I just don't want anyone to get hurt.

Purposefully oblivious, I missed that conversation and several others. I knew Dick had a Facebook account, but figured he'd never looked at it again after his grandkid helped him set it up. That was his first and last post.

While I was bar-hopping, police were questioning neighbors and friends of both Kathleen and mine. Certain

I'd had an affair, they were tearing apart my old phone, my laptop and our family desktop computer searching for anything. I hoped that when they dug deep, they'd see that some of the things that made me look bad could be explained away.

They questioned the mother of every kid on my baseball team to see if I'd accepted any blow jobs for playing time. They didn't quite word it that way, but it was implied. The one I'll never forgive is that they questioned my female students, making the entire school think I must have been up to something behind a closed classroom door.

I had always been careful, perhaps even a little too careful about the teenage girls in my classroom. That started years earlier when Jerry Painter, a lawyer from the Washington Education Association, spoke at one of the classes I was taking to become a teacher. That guy scared whatever male instinct I had right out of me.

He told stories about the obvious teacher fuckups: Young teachers who'd slept with teenage girls. They had been fired, jailed and disgraced for life. I thought: Big deal? What kind of loser would sleep with a student?

But, he continued with a bunch of gray area that terrified me.

"If a student gives you a hug, be very careful. If you touch a bra strap, that can be construed as an advance upon a student."

"Never, ever give a student a ride. You will open yourself up to accusations if the student one day decides they don't like you. They will use that to ruin your career, and not even a brilliant lawyer like me can save you."

"Never, ever get yourself stuck alone with a student. Not that I don't trust you all, but a lot of X-Rated movies start out that way. So, if your colleague walks by, they will assume you are trying to sleep with your student."

"If you would like to sleep with your student, make sure you wait until at least two years after they have graduated. Otherwise, it is assumed that you groomed that student and were simply waiting for them to turn 18."

After hearing that, I was over-the-top careful. So, when a student graduated or saw me for the first time after a summer and offered an enthusiastic hug, I backed away and gave a limp, one-armed hug. I could see that it was a little insulting, like giving a man a half-assed handshake. My door stayed open always, and I made sure that I was near it if a student came in for help alone after school.

There was cleavage everywhere. I didn't look, and I didn't enforce the dress code because I didn't want anyone to ask how I could see that they were violating it. I didn't text students, and I turned down their Facebook friend requests. Not only was I never going to cross a line; I was never going to get close enough to the line to see it.

Now students were being asked if they'd fucked their teacher, but Painter's warnings had saved my fat ass. Police quickly realized that it was a dead end since I'd never as much as smiled at a teenager. The comment from my friend Adam about an affair rattled around in their brains, but never settled anywhere.

29

More Beer

Albuquerque, New Mexico

Mallory Facebook check-in: Her name is Rio and she dances on the sand. –at Grande Brewing.

Address entered in the GPS, I sped out of the tramway parking lot. Pedestrians shot me dirty looks, but I was even more pissed at myself. It was stupid to sit in the parking lot and feel sorry for myself and Kathleen. There was nothing else near the tram, and I should have driven back toward the city instead of pouting. Now I was 15 minutes away from Grande Brewing instead of 5.

I assumed he'd used the timing of me liking his tramway check-in to figure out when to descend. Just as he had been all along, he was one step ahead of me. I decided then I would not like or comment on anything else. Hopefully I could outguess him at some point. Surprise, my only chance.

Just after Tramway Road turned into Roy Avenue, the lights of an Albuquerque Police car lit up my rearview mirror.

Panic.

Was I being arrested and soon to be extradited back to Washington state? Did the tram employee report me as a potential threat to society?

Or, was I getting pulled over for speeding, at which point the officer would learn that police in another state wanted me for questioning. I slowed and pulled to the side, leaving my hands on the wheel, in plain sight. Getting shot for looking like I was reaching for a gun would not help Kathleen.

That's when the police car sped by me, heading after someone else. I started breathing again and after a moment started toward my destination.

The GPS took me to the entrance of a trailer park just short of the Rio Grande. I nearly turned around before seeing a homemade sign on the other side of the road: Grande Brewing. I pulled in, doubling the number of cars in the lot.

Grande Brewing occupied an Adobe building that looked like it'd been abandoned long ago. An extension made of cement painted brown to look like adobe had been built to house the brewing operation. It appeared to be closed or maybe even out of business, but the door squeaked open when I gingerly pushed it. I slowly walked across the cracked cement floor and took a seat on a barstool that seemed to have a strong chance of giving way.

A woman came out of the back and offered me a warm, crooked grin. She appeared to be at least part Mexican American. Maybe Native American or a little of both. She wore a maroon shirt and khaki shorts over her brown skin, making up the three main colors of everything I'd seen so far in New Mexico.

She was not thin, but not fat. She was the type of woman who caught your eye and made you look twice. The second look was perplexing. Nothing stood out. She wasn't stunningly beautiful. She didn't have a big rack. But, despite average raw materials, the final project was, well, sexy. A complete woman much superior to the sum of her own parts.

I cursed myself for those thoughts with my wife quite possibly dead or dying.

"Hey there," she said, slowly, brown eyes looking into mine like I was the most interesting person she'd ever met. "Are you Bob?"

Ah, Jake had been the most interesting person she'd ever met. That snapped me out of my momentary fascination and any thoughts of letters to Penthouse that might have developed.

"Yeah, I'm Bob," I said, refocused.

"Your friend Chico said to take care of you," she said. "Let me get you a beer."

Nice. Chico Fraley. Another UW linebacker.

"No, I'm good."

"Chico insisted. He said you'd love the Bomb Shelter Stout."

Another clue? I was probably just being optimistic, looking for any sign that Kathleen might still be alive. I hoped this was an indication that he had her trapped in a room somewhere. Hopefully a plush bomb shelter, if such a thing existed.

"Did, uh, Chico, come in with, uh, his wife or was he alone?"

"He was alone," she said pulling on the tap handle as the dark beer slid down the inside of the glass, with a tan foam head forming.

"Did you see what he was driving?"

"No, why?"

"Oh, no reason, he's just got a really neat old Mustang," I lied. "You sure he wasn't with anyone? You didn't hear anyone?

"No, it was just him," she said, handing me the glass. "You OK, honey?"

No, I wasn't. I faked a smile, and took a sip.

"He did say to hang out here for a while, and he'd let you know what's next. Not sure what he meant by that."

"Did he look pissed when he said that? Like, really pissed?"

"No, honey," she chuckled. "He seemed like a normal guy, other than he left me a tip bigger than what I got all last week."

Chico, it turned out, had also bought me a meal. Grande's specialty was sausage made from different types of meat. I was hungry, and quickly downed bison and rattlesnake sausage. Looking around, I wasn't sure how that place passed its last health inspection, but it was tasty. I cursed my dirty mind for working on a joke that had something to do with the bartender and sausage.

Though always guilty of a dirty mind, the timing seemed inappropriate. Flat-out wrong. I felt reckless, as if I'd lost all concern for consequences.

Two hours passed. Nothing. I sat frozen, nursing a second beer. I thought about driving toward downtown. Or maybe trying my luck with another brewpub. Nothing was gained from sitting here, though I didn't see any advantage to driving somewhere else that could be even farther away from Kathleen. So I watched time tick away as I drank.

"Ma'am, mind if I ask your name?"

"It's Rio," she said.

"Rio? Really? Rio Grande? Come on."

She smiled, which I took as an admission.

"So, uh, Rio, did, uh, Chico say where he was going?"

"No, not really. He didn't say much. I think he said he was going to do some hiking. He asked me about the weather. Said he couldn't decide whether to go tomorrow, the next day or wait until the weekend."

I seethed. And, he'd played her just right. He'd used her to fuck with me.

"Look, Rio," I said, gaining some confidence as I neared the end of the second beer. "This guy is kind of screwing with me. He's running me all over town, trying to avoid me. It's a long story…"

"I've got time, honey," she said, looking around the empty bar. I knew she probably called everyone honey, but I liked it for some reason.

I told Rio that Chico–I liked that name better than Jake–had threatened my family and that I needed to talk to him.

"You're not going to do anything crazy, are you honey?" she asked, softly.

"No, no, no," I said, wishing I were lying. "I just want to talk to him."

She smiled, slightly relieved.

"Rio, I need you to listen to me, OK?" I said.

She nodded, looking at me intensely, like I was about to read her the recipe for the greatest batch of beer ever fermented. "If anyone comes here asking about me, tell them you saw me here at this time. And, if it's an emergency or something, tell them to look for me on the north trail to Wheeler Peak. Can you do that for me Rio?"

"Sure thing, honey, I can do that."

"Thanks, it's really important."

"What's this all about?"

I let the question hang in the air and dropped a $20 on the counter–big bucks for a cheapskate like me. I reversed my earlier decision and checked-in at Grande Brewing on Facebook, hopefully making Jake think I was staying there for a while. I headed south, exiting the freeway just before getting back to the Big I. I pulled into the lot of a highly rated brewpub called Canteen Brewhouse. Total wild guess.

Two more hours and another brewpub later, it became clear there was no needle in the haystack. I refreshed Jake's Facebook page incessantly. Nothing. Finally after another hour, a check-in. An odd one.

30

The House

Rio Rancho, New Mexico

Jake Facebook check in: Jake was at–The House.

The House? What the fuck was The House? I didn't know what, but I did know where. One of Facebook's check-in features is that it shows a map.

The House was located at the south end of the city of Rio Rancho, about 15 miles away. He had to just be throwing me off the scent now–not that I had picked up a scent. Was he sending me to Rio Rancho for a reason? Or some sort of diversion? I had no clue, but felt I also had no choice. Rather than develop bedsores on my ass, I decided to check it out.

Wanting nothing to do with the carpocalyptic traffic on Paseo Del Norte, I used the map on my phone to drive west on Griego, North on 2nd and west again on Montaño.

New Mexico, and Rio Rancho in particular, had to be the most camouflaged area I'd ever seen in my life. Houses, all of them fake adobe reddish brown, blended into the brown rock and dust.

I could hear Malvina Reynolds in my head, singing "Little Boxes."

Little boxes on the hillside

Little boxes made of ticky tacky
Little boxes on the hillside
Little boxes all the same

Hell, even the trees were brown. I wondered if all the sunshine was worth it. *Ask yourself that in February, after a few months of Seattle rain*, I thought. If there would be another February in my lifetime.

Pink Floyd's "One Slip" played on Albuquerque's classic rock station. I loved that song when it came out in 1987, but despite what the courts ruled it wasn't really Pink Floyd without Roger Waters. Today it sounded too much like 80s music, though I interpreted the lyrics differently as I drove toward Rio Rancho.

One slip, and down the hole we fall
It seems to take no time at all

I neared the neighborhood. It was sub-divided into half-acre lots. Built just before the housing market crash, many of the lots still sat empty. Those who built were rewarded by views of Sandia Peak, not much of a selling point for me.

The homes were so foreign to me, I didn't know if they were big or small. My Pacific Northwest wooden-house frame of reference offered no help. The vehicles parked in driveways and the occasional 3-car garage told me that there must be some decent living quarters, though many of the streets were gravel. Nice neighborhoods in Seattle did not have gravel roads.

The House was on a dead end road with only two other dwellings. They were spaced far enough apart that it was pretty clear which was the correct one from the Facebook check-in. I parked in front of a vacant lot, and slinked toward the driveway. There were no cars or people on the street that I could see.

It looked like every house I'd seen so far. Brown. Gravel driveway, with a nicer cut of rock than the road. An even better cut of rock for a yard. On high alert, I walked slowly up the driveway until I reached yet another bunch of rocks that formed a path to the front door.

I stood in the rocks for a moment. Do I ring the doorbell? Would he open the door and blow my head off into the less fortunate rocks?

After weighing my options, I moved toward the door and pushed the doorbell button.

No answer. Not even a free beer at this place.

I stepped off the path and into the yard rocks. I walked carefully around the house attempting to look in each window, but all were covered by drapes or blinds. No lights. No one cooking dinner. Not a sight, sound or smell that I could detect. I jiggled the door handles. Nothing. I even tried to pull up the garage door.

Feeling like I'd worn out my welcome, I quickened my pace back to the car. I drove a few blocks and parked. And waited, again.

I didn't know it then, but there was a dead body in that house. A few hours later, police would be looking for a stocky guy driving a gray SUV who'd been seen walking around the outside of the house. Had I known what was in there, I would have done things much differently.

31

LAST BEER

Rio Rancho, New Mexico

Mallory Facebook check-in: I'll be stumblin' around the mountain as she comes–at The Stumbling Steer.

Funny guy, that Jake. I wondered how long this was going to go on. Was I going to tour every brewery in greater Albuquerque before he put a bullet in my head? I considered not going. Maybe I should just drive up toward Wheeler now and get this over with. But, some of the stops offered some clues. If another clue existed at the Stumbling Steer, I didn't want to miss it.

Maybe he would just kill me, and somehow she would survive. That was the only reason I continued on this aimless quest. Better me than her. I wished I'd upped my life insurance so I would be worth more to her dead than alive. "Hell," I thought out loud, "then she'd probably get arrested for killing me."

It was odd, that moment when I accepted that I might die. I'd always marveled at the courage of soldiers at war. How did they throw their bodies in front of machine gun fire and dive on grenades to save others? I didn't even understand how they made it through the day-to-day war shit. Sitting in muddy trenches for days until feet became deformed. Freezing in the forests. Walking through swamps filled with disease and things with teeth that hid under the surface of murky water. I found it impossible to relate to these heroes.

As a teacher and history buff, I'd watched countless documentaries and read many books about war. How people could find courage, I never really understood until I watched *Band of Brothers* a few years back. It was a World War II documentary about American soldiers who'd performed heroics during D-Day and other parts of the war. One of the veterans put it into perspective for me in a way no one ever had before. Fifty years after parachuting into France, Ronald Speirs, who commanded "E" (Easy) Company, said, "The only hope you have is to accept the fact that you're already dead. The sooner you accept that, the sooner you'll be able to function as a soldier is supposed to function: without mercy, without compassion, without remorse. All war depends upon it."

I was no more like Ronald Speirs than Ronald McDonald was. He'd helped save the free world. I was a middle-aged, mediocre person likely on his way to accomplish nothing more than filling a hole in the ground. But, there was a part of me that understood what Speirs meant.

Perhaps overtired and using coping mechanisms, I began thinking of reasons why it would be good to be dead. First on my list was that this was October and I'd miss November. More specifically, I'd miss all the "month of thanks" bullshit on Facebook.

There were many reasons to be thankful, but those subjects often went untouched during the month of thanks. It was usually women–men rarely participated–thanking themselves in a round-about way. Or being thankful for their perfect lives.

"I'm thankful for my son Timmy. He's such a smart, well-mannered boy."

"I'm thankful for my husband. He works so hard so I can do the most important job in the world–stay at home mom."

"I'm thankful for the perspective I gained volunteering at Northwest Harvest today."

The second one had led to 57 comments-worth of all-out war between working moms and housewives. It seems the working moms wanted to do "more with their lives" and the housewives chose what they thought was more important. Total Facebook bloodbath. My wife stayed out of it, telling me that she didn't have a choice because I made jack shit teaching.

I smiled at the memory. There was some truth to that statement, I knew. But, she also just liked to give me shit. I needed shit. Especially right now.

I didn't participate in the month of thanks crap, and refused to comment or like any of it. Last November, I was mostly thankful that I'd managed to avoid ever smacking a student, even though a few of them probably deserved it. I was thankful that I'd never told Rhonda, the annoying mom, to shut her fat fucking face, even though she probably needed it and I would have been martyred by everyone in the greater unincorporated Snohomish County area.

All those thoughts quickly evaporated as I turned off Golf Course Road onto Ellison Drive. I pulled into a parking lot, greeted by a giant barrel with lighted white, old-west looking letters that confirmed I was at The Stumbling Steer Brewery and Gastropub. I had no idea what gastropub meant. It made me think of eating bad food that gave me gas, but I was pretty sure that wasn't the correct definition.

I parked and walked. Emotions of scared and sad had long departed, and only anger remained. I walked up to the brown building. Big fucking surprise, a brown building in New Mexico. I entered through the glass and wood door, and found a huge restaurant that somehow found the perfect restaurant intersection of cowboy and yuppie.

Briskly, I approached the hostess, stepping in front of a family of four, and said, "I'm looking for Brett Collins," I said, naming the only remaining starting UW linebacker from 1991 that Jake hadn't used yet. "Any chance he's here?"

"Oh, are you Bob? I was told to look for you," said Lexi, a girl in her late teens who'd been put in the front for a reason. I figured this girl's next job would be Dallas Cowboys cheerleader and then rich dude arm candy.

Brett Collins. I'd finally gotten one thing right in this maze.

"How long ago was he here?"

"About an hour ago. He said to take care of you."

"Fuck this," I muttered too loudly.

"Sir?" she said, eyes drifting to the annoyed family behind me.

"What else did he say?"

"Here, I wrote it down. Could you step aside and I'll be right with you?"

She handed me a pink sticky note that smelled like apricot jelly. In teen girl handwriting it said, "few more things u need to know meet soon."

The hostess showed me to a table. A waitress approached moments later with a beer.

"Compliments of Mr. Collins," said Jenn, the waitress.

Autopilot took over my brain for a moment, and I tried to figure her age. It surprised me how often my brain could turn away from the anxiety and horror it faced and find a few moments to be normal. Stupid normal, but normal for me.

It was hard to tell her age. She could be a really hot 42-year-old. But, she could also be a 28-year-old with a lot of miles on her.

"Awesome, what kind of beer is this?"

"Red River Ale," she said with a raspy smoker's voice that revealed her odometer. "He said you'd like it. Actually, he made some cheesy comment about how you like brunettes," she said, touching her dark hair, "but this red was extra special."

Jenn wore a tight Stumbling Steer T-shirt and a mini-skirt that showed off her firm, tan legs.

"Yeah, he thinks he's a funny guy, doesn't he? Did he say anything else?"

"No, just that he'd see you soon. He was only here long enough to take care of your meal."

"What a guy," I said. "Always looking out for me. I'm assuming he left you an excellent tip."

"Yeah, he did. I've done a lot worse things for $50."

I was pretty sure she was just being honest, but she laughed while winking and touching my shoulder. "I'm just kidding. He already ordered for you. It'll be out in a few minutes."

Jenn brought out a full rack of what the menu said were Korean Style Baby Back Ribs, complete with dragon sauce, Korean potato salad and kimchi cole slaw. It sounded horrid, and I felt more sick than hungry. Thinking I might need some energy later, I began picking at it. It was delicious, which I found annoying. This guy was playing me like a Neil Peart drum set. He even knew, better than me apparently, what kind of food I liked to eat.

"What happened to your head," asked Jenn while bringing me a second Red River Ale.

The lump remained, and a nice shiner was beginning to fill in under my eye.

"Car accident," I said. "Always buckle up."

"Oh, I'm sorry. Everyone OK?"

"Yeah, one car accident. Don't text and drive."

Jenn smiled and walked away. I ate until I was comfortably full, having to hit the brakes hard to not go past that point. I asked Jenn all the usual questions. No, she hadn't seen him with a woman or anyone else. No, he didn't say where he was going or when he'd be in touch. Just as I'd nearly decided that this was a complete waste of time, I remembered the Red River Ale. Jake had made a point of making sure I knew that was important.

I returned to the hotel from the previous night, and began my routine of waking every 30 minutes to check Facebook. My phone buzzed constantly. I did my best to avoid looking at the screen as I clicked out of messages, though one from detective Stevens reminded me of the seriousness of the situation.

We really need to talk to you right away, Mr. Peddin. We have some new information. Please call me immediately.

32

2ND AMENDMENT

New Mexico

My mother's post on my Facebook wall: "Where the fuck are you??"

I saw that one by accident at 4:30 a.m. It was a great question, though. Where the fuck was I?

"The only fucking place your wife for sure is not," I said out loud.

Giving up on sleep, I got out of bed.

"Fuck this," I said out loud before thinking, *I'm going to Wheeler Peak.*

After a quick rinse in the shower, I packed a few items and at just before 5 a.m. began a trip that seemed destined to end in disaster.

I briefly considered, but mostly ignored, all the things wrong with finding and confronting Jake.

I remembered the sign *Great Living at 10,200 feet.* That altitude had not been such great living for me. It was a struggle to walk down the street without getting winded. At Wheeler, I'd be starting at about 9,200 feet. The hike to the summit of 13,161 feet was about 8 miles. I doubted many started up that trail less prepared.

I had no idea if, when or where I'd see Jake. What if he was going all the way to the summit? How was I going to drag my fat ass up that mountain? I was out of shape with a knee missing most of its cartilage. I wasn't sure I could walk 8 miles at sea level. Now, I was going to gasp for oxygen while gaining 4,000 feet of elevation?

If I somehow made it up that mountain, what would be left of me? What was I going to do, kick the ass of someone in better shape than me after completely burning everything I had on the way up the trail?

Another very real issue was the lack of a weapon. There was a good chance that Jake was packing heat. I was packing a pocketknife. I'd considered purchasing a gun, but didn't even know how to do it. I didn't know if an alarm would go off when a murder suspect walked into a gun shop. Then there were waiting periods. And, I didn't know a shady goombah-type who could–what do kids call it these days?–hook me up.

As a U.S. History teacher, I'd sat through many gun debates. I'm not sure if it was because of so many years as a moderator, or if I was just a serial fence-sitter, but I was personally very divided on the gun issue. I'd grown up around guns and had shot them many times without issue. Of course I'd also seen all the horror guns can assist.

The debate raged on in Facebook-land as well. Every school shooting reopened the wound with moms everywhere posting things like "When will we make all of this stop? Wake up, America?" which was followed by the gun guys accusing these moms of using victims to further their political agenda. Then the moms would accuse them of being heartless bastards who care more about holding their prosthetic penises than the lives of children. I'd learned to avoid Facebook for days when something major happened. I couldn't handle the stupidity coming from either side.

There were three things I knew about guns.

1. Most people, whether vegan Volvo drivers who politely relocate spiders from their living rooms to their porches or the right-wing guy waiting for the government to turn on him, had never actually read the Second Amendment. One sentence long. Twenty-seven words. Too long, apparently to hold the attention of most: *A well regulated Militia, being necessary to the security of a free State, the right of the people to keep and bear Arms, shall not be infringed.* Like the rest of the Constitution, this can be interpreted many ways. I always figured it might help the discussion if more than seven people in the U.S. read the Amendment before ranting about it.
2. Like most things in the world, in theory, it should be all right for people to walk around with guns. It should also be OK for us to trust our sons to priests and boy scout troops. And it was, almost all of the time.
3. I was too stupid to own a gun. I was sure I'd be that guy. I'd be the dumbass who'd go to a range, come home and set my piece on the counter while getting a beer from the fridge. Bang! Oops, silly me, forgot I'd set that there. I'd be the guy who'd lock the safe every day, except that one day when my son would come home with his buddy and stumble upon the open safe. Bang! Oops, silly me, forgot this time. Sorry about your face, kid. Or, I'd be the guy who'd shoot his own kid sneaking into the house while returning from a party in the middle of the night.

So, while in theory I believed the whole "Assault rifles don't kill people. People kill people!" angle, my pragmatic side knew this was a bad idea. Most people were like me: Too stupid to own guns. That's something responsible gun owners either failed to realize or admit even if they weren't committing gun violence. I wished I could hand out the guns to the 10 percent of the population who could actually handle them. Truthfully, I felt the same about driver's licenses and human reproduction.

My guess was that Jake carried. He'd hunted from time to time, so he at least knew his way around guns. When I had thought about it I'd figured that me having a gun would ensure my death and probably Kathleen's. If I found them on the mountain, he'd certainly be expecting me and would be in a better position than me. He might have me in his sights before I even saw him at all. My only hope was to talk to him. Bargain with him somehow. Make him feel at ease. When I considered this it seemed pretty hopeless. So, I mostly didn't think about it, instead worrying about the issue surrounding even making it up the trail. I wasn't convinced I'd live long enough to be killed.

Fueled by ignorance, I left Albuquerque behind, heading North on I-25. I forced myself to stop at a gas station outside Santa Fe for some water, caffeine and granola bars. I'd need the energy for the two-hour drive toward Taos, New Mexico, and a who-the-fuck-knows-how-long hike.

At Española, I took Highway 68 as rays of yellow light slowly began to awaken the Sangre de Cristo Mountains. I felt oddly energized despite days–hell, months–with little sleep. I kept forcing myself to lay off the gas pedal, not knowing how a traffic stop of a murder suspect on the lam would end.

I could see some of the landscape now, and it reminded me of old Roadrunner cartoons. I thought of that poor stupid coyote, fruitlessly chasing a faster and smarter animal. At great personal and financial expense,

Wile E. Coyote always failed miserably, usually by falling off a cliff.

Not liking the metaphor forming in my thoughts, I began playing with the radio as I drove. I'd never used Satellite radio, but after some old man confusion at this new-fangled device, I found a classic rock station.

"Ten Years Gone" by Led Zeppelin came on the radio. I was a Zeppelin fan, but had never paid much attention to this song. I listened to the words a bit, and they stuck with me. It's funny how easy it is to make a song fit your situation at a moment in time.

I thought about what it would be like to reunite with Kathleen as Robert Plant howled:

Then as it was, then again it will be
Though the course may change sometimes
Rivers always reach the sea

The song played in my head for hours as if I'd hit the repeat button and ripped off the knob. Things don't have knobs anymore, but they still exist in my head.

I glanced over at the mountains the way a kid might look down the end of a high diving board after climbing the ladder. A single, sombrero-shaped cloud rested atop the mountain range. The Rio Grande twisted alongside, oblivious to my journey.

I crossed Embudo Creek, and passed Blue Heron Brewery and Winery.

"The one frickin' brewery in New Mexico I haven't been to yet," I scowled as Lynyrd Skynyrd provided background music.

"Yet," I said, realizing I hadn't checked Facebook lately.

I pulled to the side of the road, and checked my phone while pissing over a guardrail. Midstream, I realized that maybe I was on the right track. No free beer this time, though.

33

BIG CLIMB

Taos, new Mexico

Mallory Facebook check-in: Now we're up in the big leagues, getting' our turn at bat. As long as we live, it's you and me baby. There ain't nothin' wrong with that.–at Bull-of-the-Woods Trail.

That was a reach. Ah, Jake. The world's only cheeseball serial killer. He'd checked in a few minutes earlier, and I was less than an hour away from the trailhead. It was impossible to know how far along the trail he was or what his pace was like. I hoped it was slowed by Kathleen, though to be honest she was in better shape than me.

As I neared Taos, I was struck by the dichotomy of its inhabitants. Look to the right, a vacation cabin bigger than my house. Look to my left, a teepee. Look back to the right again, a run-down single-wide with junk–no, junk is too useful, let's call it debris–scattered all around the property.

I bypassed downtown Taos, taking Highway 240, which at some point turned into Blueberry Hill Road. I worked hard to chase that song out of my head as it had taken on a whole new meaning. I didn't want to find a thrill on any hill.

I crossed Paseo Del Pueblo Norte, not to be confused with the Paseo Del Norte cluster fuck I'd crossed in Albuquerque, and continued north on Highway 150. The Rio Hondo cut into a valley that dropped below the highway. Cottonwoods drank from the river surrounded by granite peaks that became more menacing with each mile.

The trailhead was located at Taos Ski Valley, which was in mid-October transition. Most of the hikers were done for the year. The temperatures were dropping, but ski season was still over a month away.

The ski area was not totally dead, however. White trucks driven by contractors and workers buzzed around the ski area hive as they prepared to open the place to the skiers who would drop nearly as much green on the place as the white snow that fell from the sky.

I double-checked the directions I'd found at summitpost.org and parked in a ski area overflow lot currently used by only two cars. A small Ford Ranger pickup truck was parked a few spots over from a gold, mid-70s Cadillac Eldorado with Washington plates. I cringed when I noticed the large trunk.

This was the same car I'd seen Jake with at the UW game last fall. He'd removed the purple gameday decorations from it, but this was the car. This was the place.

I froze. Could he be watching me now? No. He had to be far along the trail by now. I grabbed my backpack and found the sign to the Bull-of-the-Woods / Wheeler Peak trail.

At the trailhead, one sign explained that bighorn sheep like salt and to avoid feeding them. Another indicated that no motor vehicles were allowed, a rule I desperately wanted to break. I wondered if I should have bought a dirt bike. Then I imagined myself being shot right off the seat. I'd just have to settle for the quietness of my feet.

The weather was perfect. Low 50s and sunny, though fir trees blocked the sunlight to darken the beginning of the trail. I started jogging. That lasted about 100 yards before I began panting like a dog. "If they could just move this trail down to sea level, I might be all right," I said to only me.

The trail appeared to be well-traveled. It was rocky, but in good shape and well-marked. That helped me overcome one of my fears, that I'd be the unprepared idiot who got lost on a hiking trail.

I can do this, right? I stumbled along the tree-lined trail trying to convince myself.

I nervously navigated my way across a bridge made of tree limbs to cross a creek and marched onward. Less than a mile into the hike, I really started feeling like shit. At about 10,000 feet I was already gasping for air. My fingers felt frozen while beads of sweat formed on my forehead, a combination of overexertion and fear.

I heard a moaning sound and froze, only my eyes darting toward my right. I relaxed. It was two aspen trees swaying in the wind, rubbing together near the top as if they'd sneaked into the woods to make out.

The wind blew continuously as the elevation increased, sounding like a distant jet engine. I heard a rustling sound and stopped. Just a bird. The trail turned left, intersecting with Long Canyon Trail, then switched back to the right. A long incline stared at me now on a trail wide enough for a Jeep. Oh, how I wished for my Jeep at that moment. Magpies occasionally darted across the trail, uninhibited by the thinning air. Every sound brought a moment of panic.

Fatigue began setting in. I'd gone from jogging, to speed-walking to walking slowly to walking even more slowly and stopping every 50 feet to catch my breath. I knew I was in bad shape, but I had no idea how much I'd let myself go until walking this trail.

I remembered what I had read about altitude sickness, and felt like I might be headed toward its crippling effects. It could set in as low as 8,000 feet, and I was well above that now. I wasn't sick, but I wasn't well, either. My head hurt, I felt tired, nauseated and dizzy. Maybe it was altitude sickness, but it could also be a result of anxiety, fear, obesity and a head injury.

As I neared the next bend, with the trees slowly thinning along the widening trail, I saw a pair of aspen trees, leaves yellowing. On the left tree, years ago someone had carved TG (heart) FV. On the younger one to the right, freshly carved: JM (heart) KP.

Jake Mallory and Kathleen Peddin. Did this mean she was alive, at least?

My blood boiled. I looked around and saw nothing. I peered down into the gulley below the trail. Nothing. I climbed straight up a grassy hill to a ridge. Nothing but shortness of breath. Again, a sense of total uselessness overtook me. I sat down on a rock and tried to pull myself back together. I rested there for a few minutes as the wind howled, trying to summon an ounce of courage. It was eluding me along with Jake at that moment.

"You OK, bud?" a man's voice said.

I jumped up, reaching for but failing to find my knife.

"Whoa," he said, stepping back, hands up as if to say, *"I mean you no harm."*

"Shit, sorry," I said. "You just startled me a bit."

"No worries," he chuckled. "Name's Colton."

He took a few steps forward and stuck out a hand. I hesitated before reaching for it, concerned about my sweaty palms.

Colton, athletically built and in his mid-20s, towered over me. He wore a camo jacket, camo pants, camo hat, camo hunting boots and a camo backpack. If I had to guess, I'd bet his underwear was camo, too. The hair I could see was buzzed short, and a heavy stubble surrounded a powerful-looking jaw. Put him on the cover of a hunting magazine and the number of female subscribers would take a significant jump.

He looked at me with concerned, pale blue eyes that resembled the waters of Puget Sound on a sunny day.

"Everything OK? Need some water or anything?"

Colton had spent the night near the summit. Why, I wasn't sure. It didn't look like a round trip would faze him. Probably one of those weirdos who camped there just for fun, I thought. People do these things, apparently, but no one ever gave me an explanation that made any sense. To me, roughing it was staying in a crappy hotel in Leadville.

"No, no. I'm OK. Just needed a little break."

Colton looked me up and down, trying to figure out how I fit into the surroundings. I was as out of place here as a dolphin.

"Do you mind me askin' what happened to your head?"

I did mind, actually.

"Ah, nothin'," I said, smiling. "You should see the other guy."

He half-smiled, unsure whether or not I told the truth, and asked if I was going to the summit.

"No, I don't think so. Just going to hike a bit and head back down."

"Oh, OK," he nodded, clearly thinking it was a good thing I wasn't going all the way because I sure as hell didn't look like I was going to make it. "Make sure you drink some water and take deep breaths. It'll make you feel a lot better up here."

I nodded and reached in the bag I'd been carrying up the mountain. I found my bottle of water, unscrewed the cap and took a long pull.

"Hey, uh, Colton?"

"Yessir?"

"Anyone else on the trail today?"

"As a matter of fact, I did see one other fella up the trail. Maybe a mile. He was about as happy to see me as you were," he chuckled.

"Colton, this will sound kind of weird, but in case anything happens to me, I need you to remember that you saw me here. My name is Bob Peddin. Can you remember that?"

"Uh, yessir. You sure you're OK? You wanna walk down with me?"

I looked at Colton for a moment, a physical specimen of Jake's caliber. I wanted to ask him to come find Jake with me. But, I would never forgive myself if it got him killed. I considered asking him to send help, overruled by my fear that Jake would kill Kathleen if he sensed a posse coming. No, I would have to do this alone.

"No, I'd only slow you down. Thanks, though, Colton."

"Mr. Peddin? You'll be OK. Everything's going to be fine."

"Thanks, Colton. I appreciate that very much. I'm glad I ran into you."

After a quick, awkward wave goodbye, we parted ways. Maybe it was the adrenaline from being scared shitless, but my energy had returned. I chased an energy drink with some water and continued up the trail.

Around the next bend, I was annoyed. The trail intersected with a road. It wasn't much of a road and I didn't know where it came from, but it was a road that a 4-wheel-drive vehicle could handle with ease. I didn't see it on any map, so maybe it was private property. But, still. All this fucking hiking and I could have driven up here with ass-warmers in the Explorer.

I plodded along.

34

APB

Snohomish County, Washington

Everett Herald Facebook post: Snohomish County Sherriff's Office source says husband is person of interest in missing mom case.

By John Merton
Herald writer

A source within the Snohomish County Sherriff's Office confirmed that the husband of a missing Mill Creek-area woman is a person of interest.

The source, who requested anonymity because of the open investigation, said police would like to speak with Bob Peddin about the case of missing 47-year-old Kathleen Peddin. Police, however, have been unable to reach Bob Peddin since meeting with the 46-year-old high school teacher on Monday–one day after Kathleen Peddin disappeared from their family home on Sunday.

According to sources, police believe that Bob Peddin may have left the state. Repeated calls to Peddin have not been returned.

"We're working with other law enforcement agencies to locate Mr. Peddin," the source said.

Police have requested that anyone with information regarding the case or the locations of Bob or Kathleen

Peddin contact the Snohomish County Sheriff's Office at 425-555-1317.

I, of course, didn't see that story or the one next to it talking about community members searching the miles of wooded hiking trails that intertwined with paved roads in our large suburban neighborhood. I also didn't see all the Facebook posts and subsequent comments condemning me as a murderer loose in the streets.

35

GUILTY

Mill Creek, Washington

Rhonda, annoying mom, Facebook post: :[~ Feeling disgusted–I just cant believe he did this to her. I'm preying for her but I hope he go's to he'll.

124 people reacted to this

Debra Stone: Can't believe anyone would do anything to such a sweat person. ☹

*Debra Stone: *Sweet*

Amy Erickson: I just said a prayer for her.

Peggy Boyd: Me too, prayers.

Jennifer Sears: It's always the husband…

Bionca Stanley: OMG, what a LOOSER!!

Sonja Welch: Yep, husband. Going to he'll.

*Sonja Welch: *hell. Stupid autocorrect!!*

Mike Cohen: I say give him 30 days in the electric chair. ;)

Mickey Dobson: LOL, scary that I agree with you, Mike Cohen. I hope they fry his ass.

Deanna Riddle: I think we should all wait and hear all the facts before we judge him…

Mickey Dobson: Reeeeally Deanna? The wife's gone and the husband's gone into hiding. Guilty. Really guilty.

Sonja Welch: Agreed Mickey Dobson. Guilty.

The best part about losing phone service in the woods is that my phone stopped buzzing. Finally. I had felt a pang of guilt for ignoring it each time it rattled my thigh. It was a reminder of the two kids, other family and friends I had left behind without a word to any of them. Looking back, I wish I had trusted them more. Who knows, maybe I wouldn't have had to hike that infernal mountain. The silence of the phone, however, did add to my loneliness.

Because I ignored the outside world, I had no idea that the police noose was tightening. I could sense it a little, but could not consciously see or feel the rope.

36

MORE DEATH

Rio Rancho, New Mexico

Albuquerque Journal Facebook post: Rio Rancho Police are looking for driver of SUV for possible connection to murder of Rio Rancho man. Read our story for more information.

Man Sought for Questioning in Rio Rancho Death

By Michael Allen
Journal Staff Reporter

RIO RANCHO–Police are asking for help in finding a gray SUV that witnesses say left a Rio Rancho home where a man was later found dead.

John Mallory, 65, was discovered Monday in his home a few blocks northeast of the intersection of Unser and Westside in Rio Rancho. The cause of death has not been determined, though a source close to the Rio Rancho Police Department said the death did not appear to be accidental.

Police received a 9-1-1 call at approximately 7:30 p.m. on Monday, which led to the discovery of the body. According to a witness, a late-model, gray SUV that may have been a Ford Explorer was parked near the home. The witness saw a man described as Caucasian and under 6 feet tall with a stocky build walking around Mallory's residence a few hours before emergency vehicles surrounded the neighborhood.

"We don't know if there is a connection between the SUV and Mr. Mallory's death," police spokesperson Ken Arnold said. "We would like to speak with the driver to determine what, if anything, he might know about what occurred at the residence."

Arnold asked that anyone with any information about the SUV to contact the Rio Rancho Police Department at 505-555-5900.

Neighborhood residents say they are on high alert after a rare incident in the normally quiet suburban neighborhood.

"I just don't get it," said Dayla Braun, who lives across the street from Mallory's home. "Nothing like that ever happens around here. Maybe a car prowl or something like that, but this is unreal."

Neighbors say that Mallory was a quiet neighbor who was polite but generally kept to himself.

"I didn't really know him," said Andy Hendrickson, a neighbor. "He seemed polite, would wave if you waved at him. I can't imagine him ever doing anything that would get him killed."

Police would not say if Mallory's death was suspicious, though observers say that the police activity surrounding the scene suggested foul play.

37

Al's trail

Red River Canyon, New Mexico

Colton Facebook post: Ran into an old guy coming down from Wheeler. Dude was gassed but wasn't giving up. Inspirational!

At about 11,000 feet, I felt drunk. Drunkenness is often accompanied by stupidity and overconfidence, and apparently this also applies to lack of oxygen to the brain. Odd as it seemed, I began feeling a little better. My pace quickened with only the pain of bones in my left knee clanging together like crash cymbals slowing me.

I passed a sign for "Al's Trail" and wondered about Al. Did Al die on this trail? Did he just really like the trail so they named it after him? Did he make the trail and name it himself? Did it lead to Al's house, where he would scream "Get off my land" and fire a warning shot in the air to drive home his point?

Next up, Antoine's corner. Maybe Al and Antoine were buddies. I hoped they'd found each other out here and developed a meaningful, long-lasting friendship. I thought about this stuff to take my mind off breathing.

A slow-moving half-hour later, at or near the top of Bull-of-the-Woods Mountain, I arrived at a point where hikers would likely reach for their cameras.

A valley separated me from several peaks. Most were green, waiting to turn white with snow in a matter of weeks. Larger peaks cleared the tree line, with rocky earth looking like gray nipples emerging from fir-covered mounds. Garlands of snow, holdouts from the prior winter, decorated the mountains. A river shimmered along the bottom of the canyon.

A brown sign with white letters notified me that I was at the Red River Canyon Overlook. I took a swig of water and walked toward a second sign warning me that I was about to cross on to private property. A few feet past that, a third sign, Al's Trail. Aha, I'd reached the other end of Al's trail. Perhaps Al had dared an excursion through private property and met the wrong person.

Just as I started thinking about my wrong person, I saw something that made me freeze.

A tent. Tucked into the trees, just off of Al's trail, a small camping tent. Could this be Jake's tent? Was Kathleen in there? My oxygen-deprived brain finally kick-started, and I remember my Red River Ale from The Stumbling Steer.

"You're early," a voice farther along the ridge said.

I stopped. You could almost hear the cartoon "Wah, wah…" in the hissing wind. I brought my eyes back toward the cliff's edge, further up Al's trail, and zeroed in on a rifle pointed at my chest.

"Hi Jake," I said, matter-of-factly.

I oozed fear but tried not to show it. I had to remain calm. Just a walk in the woods to meet an old buddy.

A bright blue sky surrounded Jake, who stood a few feet in front of the edge of a cliff overlooking the canyon. The tent moved, and I heard a muffled moan. She was alive! But, for how much longer? I tried not to look, not wanting him to play my worry against me.

I felt so fucking stupid. I was like a trout drawn to a shiny lure. Oooh, look at the pretty mountains. My grand plan, if I had a plan at all, might as well be thrown into the canyon. A couple of hours earlier, I thought maybe I could sneak up on him somehow. Maybe just long enough for Kathleen to escape. It wasn't much of a plan, but it was something. Now I had nothing but certain death staring at me through sights, 20 yards away.

"I feel terrible," Jake said. "I haven't had time to prepare for company. I guess we'll just have to make the best of it."

I smiled at him. It was forced. I had to find a way to reason with him somehow, if it was possible to reason with a psychopath.

I wanted so desperately to see Kathleen. Just one more time before I died. But, the only way out of this was to get Jake talking. Make him feel comfortable. Stall and hope for a mistake on his part. That was the plan.

Yeah, that was my plan.

"You don't have a beer, do you Jake? I've had a lot of great beer the last few days and could use my fix today."

"I'm glad you enjoyed it," he said. "I figured you might as well have some fun during your last few days. Kind of like a Make-A-Wish trip."

Talking about my death wasn't quite where I wanted to go. I felt like I was driving through downtown Seattle on a rainy night, and had just turned the wrong way down a one-way street. I quickly pulled a U-turn.

"Look, Jake, I'm not here to cause you any trouble. I just want Kathleen to walk away from this. I'm here to trade. Me for her."

"You're a helluva lot uglier than her. That's the best deal you've got? I'd have to be pretty damned drunk to make that trade."

I forced a chuckle as Jake looked in my eyes. I held his gaze for a moment before looking away, like a dog who thought about going berserk but wasn't dominant enough.

If anyone could look the part of a fashionable serial-killer hiker, it was Jake. He looked like a page out of the REI catalog: *Keep warm, look great and feel comfortable while you're dragging those bodies into the woods! Want to turn heads in the streets while going unnoticed in the wild? Welcome to our wonderful world of green and brown!*

I assessed the situation, realizing he had me in every category. He held a superior weapon and was a much better physical specimen. Even though I was early, he was better prepared. He had my woman. And he dressed better. Just like high school.

"Look, Jake, I don't really give a shit about anything you've done," borrowing a line from that asshole, Detective Stevens. "I really don't," I continued. "I was curious, sure. But, I never went to the police. Never told anyone."

"I'm pretty sure you'd run your fucking mouth now. Nice try."

"We all have reasons for what we do, man. What do I care about a bunch of bitches, anyway."

I cringed when I said that. It sounded phony as hell.

"Why do you think they were bitches?" he asked, seeming genuinely curious.

"I'm just assuming, man," I said, like a subpar used car salesman trying to relate to the customer he hoped to screw over. "They probably fucked around on their husbands, treated their kids like shit. Who knows? Who cares? I'm sure you had your reasons, and I've got no issues with it at all."

Jake grinned, sizing me up.

"You're full of shit. And, stupid. I knew you'd come up here. Thanks for making my job easy."

I cringed. That sounded like a line in a movie, right before the guy pulls the trigger. In the movie, there would be someone who would gun him down just as the camera zoomed in on Jake's trigger finger pulling inward. No such luck here, but Jake wasn't shooting. Yet.

"Dude, why would I come up here? I just wanted to let you know that I've got no problem with you, OK? I'd be pretty fucking stupid to come up here and try to start something with you. Look at me, dude. You're a fucking Greek god, and I'm Jimmy the Greek. I didn't come up here for any reason other than to ask you to let Kathleen go."

"Why the fuck should I let that bitch go?"

"I think the better question is why would you not let her go?" I said, disgusted with how stupid that sounded. "There's no reason to kill her. Then you'd have to kill me, and that would be a pain in the ass. Think of the huge hole you'd have to dig for my fat ass."

Jake grinned. I was pretty sure he still planned to kill us both, but he had relaxed a little bit. The rifle still pointed in my general direction, but was down on his hip. I at least bought us a few seconds of life, such as it was.

"What I can't figure out is how the fuck you put this all together," he said. "Dumbass like you. Of all people. A nothing."

"Well, that's just it, man. I am nothing. I have no life– you know that. So, I just got curious and looked up a few things. I wasn't..."

"You're damned right about no life," he said, grin growing more maniacal.

Bad choice of words, I thought. Fix it. Dammit, fix it.

"Look man," I said trying another U-turn. "I just stumbled across it. Just stupid idiot luck."

Time to steer it back to Jake.

"It's fucking genius what you're doing," I rambled. "No one has ever done anything like it before and it can never be copied. Totally original. I just thought it was cool that I knew somebody like that. I wasn't ever going to cause you any trouble."

He relaxed again, a little.

"So, what happened to your head, there, big guy," he asked with his tongue poking hard into his cheek.

"Just ran into an old friend," I said, making him laugh.

He looked like he was considering something. Likely whether to kill me now or savor the moment a little longer. I searched for something to delay death.

Stroke the ego, stroke the ego, I thought.

"Man, I know you had it hard," I said. "It's incredible the person you've become. No one has come as far as you. You're an amazing guy. I'm jealous as hell. I wish I was built like you and had your drive. Hell, I always wished I'd been more like you, but never more than now."

"What, are you trying to ask me out or something, pussy?"

That sounded bad, but the tone was more in good fun than *time to pull the trigger*.

I laughed in an aw-shucks sort of manner. Just two old buddies having fun. Great living at 11,200 feet.

"Look at me, man," I continued. "I'm just boring as hell. I've never done one interesting thing in my life. You've accomplished so much. And, think about all the great things there are for you to see and do in this world. I wish I could join you, but I'd never be able to keep up."

The wind picked up a bit, feeling icy against my underdressed skin. It sounded like a waterfall tumbling over rocks.

"You know too much shit about me anyway," Jake said.

Oddly, he wasn't talking about all the lives he'd destroyed. No, his childhood memories loomed larger than murder.

"It's always bothered me that I told you too much stuff. No one else knows about any of that."

"I know, man. I never told anyone. It's OK to trust me, man. You can trust me now, too. Always. I never told anyone anything. I would never do that to you. It wasn't right, what you went through back then. It wasn't right. I know you wish you hadn't told me, but I'm glad you did. I care, man."

Stop saying, "man," I thought to myself.

"Doesn't matter now," he said. "It's all over. All over. And you did it!"

"What, um, what did I do exactly, Jake?"

I feared the answer, which I figured came along with a bullet to my temple.

"Ah, Mr. Curious again. You'd live a lot longer if you asked fewer questions."

"I know, I know. Never could keep my mouth shut. So, what did I do?"

He waited a moment, enjoying seeing me sweat it out. Truthfully, I didn't really care much what he thought I did unless it directly affected Kathleen's survival chances. His smirk worked its way toward a proud grin.

"You killed my father," he announced.

"Huh," I coughed. "I don't remember killing anyone recently."

For the first time, I found a way to control my body language. I had to make Jake believe that nothing bothered me, even his hobbies.

"Police are looking for you now, dumb fuck. You killed your wife. And, then, for some reason you decided to randomly kill some guy in Rio Rancho."

"Rio Rancho?" I stalled.

"Yeah, people saw you poking around a house in Rio Rancho. Police got an anonymous tip."

"Gee, wonder where that anonymous tip came from?" I asked sarcastically, trying to show appreciation for his genius.

"And, I just bet you were dumb enough to walk around that house and look guilty."

I forced another smile. "Good one."

"Two birds with one stone. Though it doesn't really matter since they'll never be able to arrest me anyway. You know what's really funny?"

We have very different definitions of what constitutes funny, I thought but didn't say.

"You were just a few feet away from her," he said, pointing to the tent. "She was in the bomb shelter the whole time. That was one paranoid fucker, my old man. Who builds bomb shelters?"

I took a step and stumbled. Rocks of various sizes littered the uneven ground.

Jake took a couple of steps toward me. Even with the mountains behind him, he looked like doom. He stood a few feet from the dropoff into the canyon as if inserting himself into the last Facebook profile photo I'd ever see of him.

To my left, I saw a stump that looked as inviting as my La-Z-Boy recliner. A baseball-sized quartz rock sat atop it–a forgotten souvenir from a previous hiker.

"Hey, Jake, you mind if sit down for a minute? I'm really wiped out."

"Sure, take a load off. Enjoy the view while you can."

I sat on the stump. I didn't bother to move the rock–this probably sounds ridiculous but I didn't want someone to miss it if they came back for it–so the edge of the bark jabbed at my butt cheek. Still, it felt good to sit. My legs needed the break, even though they may have been moments away from a permanent rest.

"Pretty amazing, view, huh?" Jake asked, awkwardly.

"Yeah, it is. Definitely worth the hike."

It was difficult to read Jake. He'd clearly gone off the deep end. This wasn't smooth, calm Jake. He was like high-speed bi-polar Jake. Ready to kill me one moment. Ready to die the next. Then the old, cool Jake would show up for a moment. I needed that guy. The other versions of Jake would give me no chance of saving Kathleen.

"I love hiking in the mountains," he said, eyes wandering through the valley below. "I love hiking alone. The trail doesn't give a damn what you've done or what's been done to you. It just wants to challenge you to be your best in that moment."

Oh boy, a future motivational speaker! Inspire me, Jake!

"Uh, yeah, totally dude," I said, wondering when I'd gone from used car salesman to surfer. "I've really enjoyed this hike. I could get into this."

If I make it out of here alive, I'm not even going to look at a fucking mountain, I thought.

"Yeah, that's too bad," he said, body relaxing but words tensing.

Still looking out at the valley, he said, "It's too bad you had to figure all this out. Even though you weren't exactly my kind of guy, I always thought you were a pretty decent person. I probably should have just finished you off quickly instead of putting you through all this crap. Kind of a douche move on my part."

Douche move. Yeah, bro, you could say that. Because of him, I was pretty much indirectly killing my wife and myself and bankrupting my family all while being suspected of two murders. Yeah, kind of a douche move. Definitely a violation of the bro code. I would certainly make a note of it.

I knew, then, though, that there was no bargaining. Both Kathleen and I were going to die. While I'd softened him a little, I might as well have been the Red River flowing through the canyon. It was going to take millions of years to carve through his desire to end us, and I had at best 5 minutes. The only thing keeping me alive, I figured, is that I'd been early and this didn't quite fit his timeline.

I thought about Speirs from *Band of Brothers*, and I felt it. That feeling of already being dead. I accepted it. Something about it felt warm and comforting, like a mother hugging a toddler. I was a dead man, and oddly I felt better dead than I had alive in the past week.

When you're dead, you have nothing to lose. Images of mothers now dead because of Jake crashed through my mind. Children crying. Husbands crying, some probably from jail. I saw Kathleen smiling at me. She was just like the ones he'd killed. A good person who impacted the world in a small, but beautiful way.

I thought about the mothers he hadn't killed yet. Montana, Idaho, California, Washington, Alaska. He was coming for them. He would color in his stupid high points map on Facebook, and then what? High points, World Edition?

I visualized Mason and Annie at their mother's funeral. Orphans. No mother making them smile just a little longer for the cheesy, living room prom photo. No one to accept the roses youth baseball and softball players give out on Mother's Day.

I felt a fierce rage, and an inferno in my gut as he stared into the sky. This had to end. There could be no more motherless children because of this well-dressed douchebag.

Accepting my own death, my fingers tightened around the rock behind my back. I jumped up like a catcher throwing to second to nail a baserunner trying to steal. As he turned around from the canyon, I pulled my arm back and fired, aiming for his chest. Just like when I tried to pitch in high school, the rock sailed a little high as I charged.

My high fastball hit Jake just outside his left eye, not far from where his elbow hit my head in Albuquerque. Knocked backward but still 5 feet away from the edge of the canyon he reached toward the gun he had fumbled, looking like Velma searching for her glasses in a Scooby-Doo cartoon. As he reached toward the gun I plowed into him, and we both tumbled into the canyon as dead men.

38

Canyon Tour

Red River Canyon, New Mexico

Taos Ski Valley Facebook status: Attention mountain crews and recreationalists, Taos Ski Valley is currently closed due to police activity at Bull-of-the-Woods Mountain. Please check back for updates.

I watched Jake land on his head along the side of the canyon just as my left shoulder bounced off the side of a juniper tree, gravity still pulling fiercely. I skittered around, like a bad fall during an ice skating routine. My right leg slammed into a fir tree, causing pain that felt like lightning streaking up to my knee. The impact slowed me considerably but I spun around yet again, catching hold of some brush above a steeper drop. I came to a stop and found a way to breathe.

I had no idea how far Jake had tumbled. I'd hit him in the chest with my left shoulder, causing him to fall a little to the left of where I'd gone over. After seeing his head hit, I'd been distracted by my own near death. I began to move, bit hard by both my lower leg and my shoulder. I gritted my teeth to stop from screaming and looked deeper into the canyon.

I saw nothing but green trees mixed in with brown rocks and bushes. No Jake.

I wasn't dead, but I was injured. And, no one was coming to save me. I had to climb back up the side of the canyon or die. Honestly, death didn't sound too terrible. Then, I thought about Kathleen, likely bound and gagged in that tent. Hopefully still alive, but for how long?

I assessed the damage. Something was broken on my right leg, either ankle or lower leg. My left shoulder also didn't feel right. I pulled on the brush with my right arm while pushing my left big toe into the crusty canyon surface and moved a few inches.

I worked my way to the top side of the brush, thanking it for saving me at least temporarily. I looked up. I had free-fallen about 15 feet and tumbled about another 20 feet. It was very steep and footing was questionable, but it at least looked slightly possible. I'd find out soon enough. Either I'd pull myself up to the ledge, or I'd have a high school reunion at the bottom.

It was slow going with just two fully functional limbs. My right leg was completely useless. My left arm could be used sparingly as long as I could handle some searing pain.

Broken clavicle, I thought. I'd broken it once before when I was a freshman in college while playing drunken football at 2 a.m. in Husky Stadium. Sober and older, this seemed to hurt more.

Like an idiot, I looked down and nearly passed out. Still no sign of Jake, but greenery obscured the view. I turned my head back up just as my left foot slid through crumbling rock. I started sliding down the edge, arms flailing like a spider being washed down the drain. The brush saved my life yet again.

I chose a better path for my second attempt, giving away some time and more lateral movement for the security of trees and better footing. It felt like hours later, but I reached the top. I picked up the rifle and used it as a cane and hopped along Al's trail and zipped the tent open.

I saw her and we both started shaking from crying so hard. I hugged her and kissed her, too hard.

I stopped suddenly.

"Fuck, what am I doing?" I pulled the pocket knife out of my pants and cut the zip ties binding her arms and legs. I put my hand on the side of her mouth and paused. We both cringed, and she nodded. I peeled off the duct tape in one motion while using my bad arm to try to keep her lips from coming off with the tape.

We hugged and bawled, rocking back and forth. After a minute, I pulled back and gave her a onceover. She looked OK. She hadn't been beaten. Her speech, though, was slurred. She'd been drugged and was alert but groggy.

"Peddin!!" a screaming voice from far away cut through the mountain wind. We both froze.

"Guh," Kathleen muttered. "ha-has a guh."

I glanced at the rifle sprawled halfway into the tent.

She shook her head. "No, hand guh," she slurred as her hand formed a finger gun.

"Peh-din!!!" Jake screamed again.

I limped to the outside of the tent.

"Whyyyyyyyy?"

It was a high-pitched, Tonya Harding-like scream coming from a good distance down the canyon. He sounded a bit off, either because he'd lost his mind altogether or suffered a head injury. I wondered how far he'd made it back up. How banged up was he and how long would it take him to reach the top?

"You piece of shit! I'm going to fucking kill you, motherfucker!!"

I considered my options. I could take the rifle to the edge. I would hold the advantages of aiming a rifle and standing on high ground versus his handgun from down below. He would have the advantage of knowing what the fuck he was doing and being a superior human speciman. The injury situation was an unknown variable. He didn't sound quite right, but I didn't know if that was good or bad.

"Peh-din!!"

I considered my options, and decided we would have to go for help. We had a sizable head start. But, was there a place where the canyon intersected with the trail? Could he take a shortcut? Did the road that intersected with the trail lead to him? Why didn't I have a map? Why hadn't I paid more attention to the area's geography?

"Where is he?" Kathleen asked, eyes wide and a little more alert.

"He fell into the canyon. Pretty far. It's going to be OK, but we should get moving. Are you OK to walk?"

I decided against trying to shoot Jake, probably because I was too much of a chicken shit to confront him again. I began pulling her up, pain shooting through my clavicle. Though halfway out of it because of whatever that fucker had fed her, she was in better shape to walk.

"Peddin!! I'm going to kill you, you fucking asshole!! Why did you do this to me?"

He sounded desperate, devastated. Child-like.

Well, because you were going to kill my wife. And me. And some other women. *Sadly, you might still have your chance*, I thought.

I grabbed hold of Kathleen. I'm not sure if I held her up or if she was keeping me upright. We wobbled along Al's Trail, and turned to the right down the main trail. I couldn't remember where I'd lost cell reception. At least a mile, I thought. This was going to be one fucking long mile.

"Pehhhh-diiih-hin-hin!" he wailed, broken-hearted-like, reminding me that a mile was better than sticking around.

Kathleen looked at me, slightly less terrified and sobering quickly. Though she'd never so much as smoked a joint in her life, she somehow looked like a determined stoner.

"Fucking kih-hih-hil youuuuuu," he cried, not sounding like the threat he was before the tumble. He sounded pathetic, the way I probably sounded to him all those years.

I could barely hear him now. We'd put some distance between us, and the wind rushed through sounding like a 747. Actually, it sounded a little different this time.

Like, an ATV.

An ATV!! Around the corner, a Polaris carrying two deputies with guns drawn left a dusty wake.

A gunshot sounded from Jake's direction.

39

The End

Taos News Facebook post: Sheriff says a man died from a gunshot near Taos Ski Valley. Click the link below for more details.

Man Dead of Gunshot Wound Near Taos S.V.

By Paul Archipley
Staff writer

TAOS SKI VALLEY–A man died of an apparent gunshot wound earlier today after an altercation on a hiking trail near Taos Ski Valley according to the Taos County Sheriff's Department.

Police have not yet identified the victim, though it is believed that the victim is not a local resident.

The shooting occurred on the Bull-of-the-Woods trail, a popular hiking spot that begins at Taos Ski Valley and ends at the summit of Wheeler Peak. Police say the altercation took place approximately 2.5 miles from the trailhead and ended with a fatal gunshot.

It was not clear whether or not those involved knew each other or met along the trail. Police did not say how many the incident involved, or if there were others along the hiking trail when the victim died. According to witnesses, one man and one woman left the scene in ambulances. Both appeared to be alive.

A source close to the Sheriff's Department indicated that police may have been alerted to a potential conflict and were already en route prior to the shooting. The source also said that one of the men involved in the altercation was wanted for questioning in connection to another crime in Rio Rancho.

Police said the identity of the victim will be released once his identity is confirmed and family is notified.

Old Jake had been in pretty bad shape after the fall, suffering from multiple broken bones, and a severe head injury that likely would have killed him within hours. Maybe even minutes. The final head injury, resulting from him firing his pistol into his temple, killed him much more quickly. Some believed he'd wanted to go on his own terms, which is why he pulled the trigger when he realized the end was approaching.

When the ATV rounded the corner, I was of course relieved, even as they screamed, "Get down on the ground," and pointed guns at both of us.

Once out of imminent danger, though, I wondered where things were headed. Thankfully, Kathleen's living body was evidence that I hadn't killed her. But, Jake ended up at the bottom of the Red River Canyon somehow. And, someone matching my description had been spotted poking around another death, Jake's dad. Maybe police would think I killed him while trying to kill Jake. Those thoughts flashed through my mind, but honestly all I cared about was Kathleen, and that our kids would have a mother. Hopefully, they'd visit me in prison.

Many more ATV's followed the first one. Sheriff's deputies and later the Sheriff himself and finally New Mexico State Police detectives.

They all had a lot of questions for me both on the trail and later at the hospital.

Why was I on the trail?

Who was on the trail first, him or me?

Why was Kathleen there?

Where did I think Kathleen had been for the past four days?

Why didn't I contact police?

Some of it was difficult to explain. It didn't take long for me to figure out, though, that I was no longer a wanted man.

The Snohomish County District Attorney had asked the Sheriff's Office to look into Jake the day before. It turned out there were enough patterns there to make them curious. They were watching my phone records and my Facebook account, which led to them contacting the Albuquerque Police.

Colton, the hiker I'd met along the trail, grew more and more concerned as he walked toward Taos Ski Valley. He'd talked to a forest ranger who'd called a deputy he knew. All that led them to us. Good thing. As hard as it was to get up that hill, it was an even longer way down.

Though many more questions would lie ahead, I could sense that, thankfully, I'd never get to meet Keith Morrison, at least not as a murder convict.

It would take a long time for Kathleen to mostly get over her four days with Jake. Physically, she'd fared much better than me, but it had been a scary trip. I knew she would get there, though, when at the hospital she looked in my eyes and said, "Well, Keith. It seems it wasn't the husband this time."

www.ingramcontent.com/pod-product-compliance
Lightning Source LLC
Chambersburg PA
CBHW030824310726
48980CB00006B/621/J

* 9 7 8 0 5 7 8 2 3 1 9 5 2 *